MW00640042

KRISTEN

Book Nine in the Apron Strings Series

OTHER BOOKS IN THE SERIES

Polly by Naomi Musch

Nellie by Amy Walsh

Priscilla by Jenny Knipfer

Beatrice by Patti Wolf

Joann by Donna Jo Stone

Cynthia by Jessica Marie Holt

Renee by Sandra Ardoin

Cassie by Lisa R. Howeler

Paige by Regina Walker

Maddie by Dawn Kinzer

Copyright © 2024 by Dawn Klinge

Genevieve Publishing

https://www.dawnklinge.com

All rights reserved. No part of this publication may be reproduced, distributed, or transmitted in any form or by any means, including photocopying, recording, or other electronic or mechanical methods, without the prior written permission of the publisher, except in the case of brief quotations embodied in critical reviews and certain other non-commercial uses permitted by copyright law.

Publisher's Note: This is a work of fiction. Names, characters, places, and incidents are a product of the author's imagination. Locales and public names are sometimes used for atmospheric purposes. Any resemblance to actual people, living or dead, or to businesses, companies, events, institutions, or locales is completely coincidental.

Scripture quotations are from The ESV® Bible (The Holy Bible, English Standard Version®), © 2001 by Crossway, a publishing ministry of Good News Publishers. Used by permission. All rights reserved.

Book Layout by Samantha Fury

Cover design by Samantha Fury

Kristen/ Dawn Klinge. -- 1st ed. ISBN: 978-1-7346434-4-2

Other Books by Dawn Klinge

Historic Hotels Collection
Sorrento Girl
Palmer Girl
Biltmore Girl

Novella
America's Favorite Christmastown

Dedicated to Janice,
my mom,
the first person who encouraged me to share my stories.

Our soul waits for the Lord; He is our help and our shield." - Psalm 33:20

From Mrs. Canfield's Cookery Book

Dear Friends,

How glad I am that this cookery book has made its way into your hands. I hope it will become more than a collection of recipes and that in your home, it will help foster an environment filled with love, family, friends, and of course, good food. Cooking and baking are more than necessary skills for a homemaker. They can be an art form. They can be a ministry. Most of all, they can be a way to show love.

Food is an essential and everyday part of our lives, but it can be so much more. I hope through the pages of this book you will find not only instruction but also inspiration for your body and your soul.

Happy cooking and baking! May you give and receive many blessings through your efforts.

Warmly,

Mrs. Clara Canfield

CHAPTER ONE

The air crackled with the invisible buzz of hard-earned achievements, and as the final triumphant notes of "Pomp and Circumstance" reverberated through the hallowed halls of accomplishment, Kristen Borstad and her fellow classmates took their seats. Ensconced in the front row, Kristen strained to stay engaged, the frigid metal folding chair beneath her offering no solace against the tumult of emotions coursing through her.

President Hoover stepped forward, his words resonating through the vast Kibbie Dome like a solemn anthem. "Good evening. Welcome to the University of Idaho's 2002 commencement ceremony." The weight of his words hung in the air, a proclamation that marked the culmination of years of dedication, late-night study sessions, and the relentless pursuit of knowledge.

While the president spoke, Kristen wrestled with a flood of memories. Two years ago, at her initial graduation, Kristen had grappled with the uncertainty of what lay ahead with a bachelor's in English and watched with a touch of envy as the graduate students adorned with velvet-trimmed hoods strode forward to claim their diplomas. The simple honor cord around her neck had seemed painfully inadequate.

She'd taken the scenic route through university, pausing several semesters to travel abroad, all the while yearning for answers to the existential questions about her life's purpose. Her family, a supportive backdrop in the crowd of well-wishers, had been there to offer congratulations, endure the endless speeches, and capture countless pictures. Kristen couldn't shake the guilt that gripped her—her parents had made the journey from Seattle to attend her graduation when she had no inkling of what she was going to do with her degree, let alone her life. Hence, she chose to linger in academia, chasing the elusive clarity a 'master's degree might bestow.

Even now, at her 'master's ceremony, the shadows of doubt persisted, casting a looming specter as she compared herself to her accomplished younger sister, Amy, the beacon of success at Stanford. If only she possessed Amy's relentless drive and determination. Everyone was genuinely proud of Amy and hailed her as the Borstad sister destined for greatness. Kristen, in moments of self-reflection, oscillated between labeling herself a late bloomer and an embarrassment to her family—a sentiment that weighed heavily on her.

Today, Kristen donned the coveted hood with a white velvet edge, a tangible symbol of her mastery of English literature. But this time, her parents were in Palo Alto, witnessing her sister's triumph at Stanford. Yellow roses had arrived that morning at Kristen's apartment, accompanied by yet another apology for their absence, though Kristen had repeatedly reassured them of her understanding. She understood that it was Amy's time to shine, particularly since she had a job waiting for her at Lehman Brothers in New York City. Amy's achievement was a celebration in its own right, while Kristen still awaited responses from the publishing houses to which she'd fervently applied.

The sound of Kristen's name being announced snapped her back to the present moment. It was time. She walked up the steps, a smile carefully affixed to her face, and shook hands with the president and the dean, who presented her with the culmination of her academic journey. Her smile became genuine as she heard her friends whooping and hollering, a vibrant reminder of the positive aspects of Kristen's life amid the uncertainties.

Following the ceremony, Kristen found herself picking confetti out of her hair, a task that mirrored the chaotic, unpredictable nature of her future. As she hugged several classmates goodbye, she wondered if their paths would cross again in the vast expanse beyond the familiar college town. The girl who'd shared the last two hours seated on her right nodded toward Kristen, a polite smile gracing her face as she asked, "Where are you off to next?"

"I'll be on my way to Seattle in the morning. How about you?" Kristen's response, though technically true, served as a veiled evasion of the deeper inquiry into her future career plans. Seattle beckoned, offering a brief respite with family before she returned to Moscow, Idaho, to work at Mary's Bookshop and await clarity for her future, all the while grappling with the weight of anticipation and the ever-present shadow of uncertainty that clung to her like a relentless companion. Waiting—it was perhaps the most challenging endeavor of all.

***

The last time Kristen had graced the familiar threshold of her childhood home was over Easter weekend, a couple of months ago. It was then her parents had begun to turn up the pressure, encouraging her to make some decisions about the future. She recalled how uncomfortable she'd felt, being unable to give them any answers.

Kristen parked her aging Jetta on the tree-lined street, engaging the parking brake to prevent an inadvertent descent down the steep hill. The day unfolded in the embrace of a breathtaking spring panorama. The magnolia tree in front of the two-story house stood resplendent in full bloom. Kristen hadn't lived here in eight years, yet nothing about her parents' abode had altered in that span of time. Richard Borstad, her father, was a steadfast custodian of their home who still repainted the forest green shutters on the white Cape Cod-style home every two years. Her mother, Betsy, was a paragon of domestic grace. With each changing season, she changed the wreath on the front door—its current iteration, a simple boxwood creation.

Their house was in a neighborhood where the echoes of children's laughter lingered, and neighbors exchanged warm waves. Kristen sighed, a symphony of emotions coursing through her as she opened her car door. At twenty-seven, she found herself still entangled in the wheels of uncertainty, returning without any tangible victories to share.

Before Kristen could retrieve her bag from the trunk, her father eagerly opened the front door of the house, mirroring the unspoken anticipation in Kristen's heart. "Kristen! Hey, honey. How was the drive?"

"Hey, Dad! Not bad. Long. But I'm here now! How was the trip to California?"

"Good, good. We had some beautiful weather while we were there." He paused, enveloping her in a warm hug. "The ceremony was long … lots of speeches. We just got back this morning. Your mother and sister aren't here right now. They went to the grocery store to pick up some food for brunch tomorrow." He smiled. "I was just watching the Mariners game. You can join me!"

He relieved Kristen of her bag and carried it into the house, placing it down in the front hallway. Phoebe, their faithful German Shepherd, greeted her with affectionate licks.

"Hey, Phoebe."

Kristen scratched the dog's back, stealing a moment to glance into the living room. A recent addition caught her eye—a new couch, pristine in its mid-century design yet sharing the same white hue as its predecessor, the oversized sectional. The TV buzzed with the sounds of a Mariners game, a comforting reminder of the familiar.

"There's some pie in the kitchen if you want, and I just made a fresh pot of coffee," her dad announced as he settled into the couch, the game reclaiming his attention. Phoebe joined him, a picture of contentment.

Kristen headed to the kitchen and selected a mug from the cupboard. As she poured herself a cup of coffee, her mother and sister entered through the garage door, laden with bags of groceries.

Amy deposited her belongings on the counter, embracing Kristen. "Congratulations, graduate!"

"Thanks. You too! Are you excited about your big move? New York!"

"Yeah, I just signed a lease on a place I haven't even seen yet. Hopefully, it's not a dump. I'm trusting someone named Stan—a relocation agent with the investment firm who promised me it was a steal. He said I'd be kicking myself if I didn't jump on it."

"That's awesome! When do you leave?"

"Two days…Monday. Any word yet on your job search?"

"No, not yet." Kristen shrugged, attempting to downplay her concerns.

"Come join me in New York! It would be more fun with you there."

Kristen shrugged noncommittally, then redirected the conversation. "Hi, Mom."

"Hey, honey," her mom said, embracing her while still holding a carton of eggs. "We have reservations at Canlis for seven tonight. I hope you brought something nice to wear. I thought we'd celebrate both of you girls and your accomplishments."

"Sounds like fun."

Betsy smiled and removed her heeled pumps, arranging them with precision by the back door. Kristen took in her mom's silk shirtdress, complemented by a cashmere cardigan casually draped over her shoulders. This was her grocery store attire? Kristen shouldn't be surprised; her mother, though not working outside the home, epitomized grace, elegance, and accomplishment. A dedicated volunteer on various charity boards, she wielded influence in the community.

Kristen glanced at her own attire—Birkenstocks, ripped jeans, and a faded Dave Matthews Band concert tee. Nudging Amy, she whispered, "Do you have an extra dress I could borrow tonight?"

***

The restaurant's windows framed a picturesque view of a dozen tiny white sailboats dancing gracefully along Lake Union, a sight familiar to Kristen from her childhood summers spent at the local sailing school. A smile graced her lips as she recalled the sweet simplicity of those bygone days, where hours on the water felt like fleeting moments.

Canlis, with its unrivaled view and delectable fare, offered a panorama of the city that Kristen's family reserved for special occasions. 'Between Amy and their mother, both high achievers, there had been quite a few celebratory dinners eaten at this very table.

"Kristen, why don't you apply to law school?"

Her mother's sudden suggestion interrupted Kristen's gaze over the lake. She shifted her attention, meeting her mother's gaze as she methodically buttered a dinner roll. Kristen knew better than to assume it was a casual remark. "Law school? I don't know ...."

"Even if you do get one of those editing jobs you applied for, the pay leaves so much to be desired. Just think about it."

"Okay." Kristen took a sip of water. "I'll think about it."

Going back to school was the last thing Kristen desired, yet she would utter whatever was necessary to deflect the topic. Catching her sister's eye across the table, she silently sought assistance.

Amy nodded and picked up the wine menu. "Look, they have a Beaulieu Vineyards Cabernet Sauvignon on the menu. I visited that winery when I went to Napa Valley last year. Let's get a bottle!"

As the evening continued to unfold, the weight of Kristen's perceived inadequacy lingered beneath the surface, a subtle but palpable undercurrent. Between bites of exquisitely prepared dishes, the conversation meandered through Amy's impending move to New York, her high-powered job waiting at Lehman Brothers, and the vibrant excitement of city life. Kristen listened, a silent participant in a narrative that seemed to glide effortlessly over the hurdles she faced. As the waiter poured the Cabernet into crystal glasses, the room bathed in the warm glow of the setting sun, casting long shadows that mirrored Kristen's internal struggle.

Her mother's gaze, though fond, carried an expectation that hung heavy in the air. "Kristen, dear, I hope you're not selling yourself short. There's so much you can achieve with your talents. Law school is just one option. Have you considered pursuing a Ph.D. in literature? Teaching, perhaps?"

The suggestion struck Kristen like a chord out of tune. The prospect of more years immersed in academia felt like an echo of the past, a cyclical dance that had yet to lead her to the clarity she so desperately sought. Her fork hesitated mid-air, the morsel of seared salmon poised between plate and mouth.

Amy, sensing Kristen's discomfort, interjected with a bright smile. "Mom, let's not turn this into a business meeting. Kristen just earned her Master's degree, and she deserves to enjoy her accomplishment. Cheers to my brilliant sister!"

The clink of glasses brought momentary relief, the celebratory effervescence mingling with the delicate fragrance of the flower arrangement on the table. Yet, beneath the surface, Kristen grappled with the persistent doubt that her achievements truly measured up to the standards set by her family or even herself.

The conversation drifted to safer shores, but the subtle tension persisted, a silent reminder that Kristen's journey was still a path winding through the thickets of uncertainty.

Later that night, back in her childhood bedroom, Kristen paused in front of the mirror to look at the reflection of a woman caught between two worlds. The silk fabric of the borrowed dress clung to her, a stark contrast to the casual, loose clothing she usually wore. The incongruity seemed to represent the juxtaposition of the many roles she navigated— daughter, sister, recent graduate, and woman; a woman yearning to define herself on her terms.

She quickly slipped on jeans and a T-shirt and descended the staircase. In the dim glow of the living room, Kristen joined the family circle. A question lingered: Did Kristen Borstad truly believe she was enough?

Her sojourn with her family in Seattle lasted a quick two days before she returned to Moscow, Idaho.

CHAPTER TWO

Kristen delicately trailed her fingers along the meticulously curated CD collection adorning the bookshelf. "What do you feel like listening to, Sarah?"

A distant reply came from the kitchen. "How about Coldplay? Is that good cooking music?"

"Sure, that will work." Kristen inserted the Coldplay disc and pressed play, the melodic tunes weaving through the apartment like a familiar embrace. "Are we six people tonight?"

"Yeah, everyone's coming. It's Mike, Todd, Jason, Michelle, Leah, Tori, and us."

Kristen joined Sarah, who was deftly chopping tomatoes for a salad. Kristen opened the fridge and retrieved a package of steaks. "It's probably about time to get these on the grill," she said.

The two roommates, who shared a bond forged through sorority sisterhood, had created a sanctuary within their little two-bedroom apartment near campus. Their dwelling consisted of half of the first floor of a pre-WWII-era, two-story brick walk-up that boasted charming art-deco touches. The decorative living room windows featured leaded glass and geometric patterns that never failed to elicit admiration from visitors. Despite the apartment's cozy size, Kristen and Sarah loved hosting dinner parties, occasionally squeezing as many as ten people around their table.

Sarah, with a few credits to finish in the fall, was embarking the following morning on a summer of Australian exploration, while Kristen was seriously considering her sister's invitation to move to New York City. It felt like the conclusion of a cherished chapter that Kristen would have preferred to extend. Tonight was possibly the last hurrah for the roommates as joint hostesses, and they both wanted to serve their guests a delicious and unforgettable meal.

As Kristen reached for the steak seasoning, she sank into contemplation, her thoughts drifting until Sarah playfully slapped her with a dishtowel, bringing her back to the present. "Who knows," Sarah said, "maybe we'll get one more year of living together. You don't have to leave, right? You can do whatever you want now, Grad Girl. Is moving to New York really what you want?"

"Ha, ha, right! You don't think I've been in Moscow long enough?" Kristen paused. "Although, my mother thinks I should apply to law school. That would keep me around even longer."

Sarah quirked an eyebrow as she placed a pan of rolls on the counter. "You want to go to law school?"

"No, but I told her I'd think about it. I'm still hoping to land an editing job in New York."

"And that would make you happy?"

"I don't really know. It just seems like a logical next step. I can't work at the bookshop forever, right?"

Sarah appeared on the verge of saying something as the doorbell chimed. Kristen opened the door, welcoming Mike and Michelle, their neighbors from across the hall. Michelle handed Kristen a bottle of wine, expressing gratitude for the enticing aroma wafting from the kitchen.

Todd, Jason, Leah, and Tori arrived together a few minutes later. Laughter and camaraderie flowed effortlessly among the old friends who had weathered the revolving door of friendships in a college town. Their own inevitable farewells hung in the air, but on this night, they were united. And for that, Kristen felt an overwhelming sense of gratitude.

Tori offered her assistance in the kitchen. "Is there anything I can do to help?"

Sarah handed her the bottle of wine. "Here, you can open this."

When dinner was ready, Kristen and Sarah plated a simple but delicious feast that was sure to please—steak, mashed potatoes, green salad, and dinner rolls—and everyone converged at the table. Their conversation meandered, reaching a poignant juncture when the topic shifted to family origins.

Todd, setting down his glass, turned to Kristen. "Borstad … is your last name Swedish?"

"Close, it's Norwegian. My grandparents still live in Norway. I love going to visit them; I really need to go back soon. It's been two years since I've seen them."

Tori reached for the last dinner roll. "Is your mom Norwegian, too? How did your parents meet?"

"No, my mom grew up in Seattle. She met my dad when she was traveling after college."

Sarah, gathering dinner plates, interjected, "Her mother is a Leland."

Kristen winced as recognition flashed across her friends' faces. The Leland family was a name known worldwide for their chain of upscale hotels. Why did Sarah have to disclose that information now after all these years?

Jason, handing his plate to Sarah, turned to Kristen. "Must be nice."

Though Jason's remark wasn't meant to hurt, it stung. 'Kristen had heard versions of that comment throughout her life, prompting her to keep the Leland part of her family background discreet. Once people knew her grandfather's identity, assumptions ensued, and she felt the weight of added expectations to live up to the family name. Determined not to let the comment ruin her evening, Kristen smiled and moved to bring a plate of brownies to the table.

Jason picked up on the tension. "Hey, I apologize. I didn't mean it that way."

"No worries. Hey, believe me, it's not like most people imagine. My parents didn't just give me whatever I wanted. They made me work hard for everything."

Leah reached across the table, placing her hand over Kristen's. "Hey, you're one of the hardest working people we know. You don't have to convince us."

***

Kristen diligently arranged the dishes in the dishwasher, the clinking of glassware the only noise in the kitchen. Meanwhile, Sarah extinguished the candles scattered around the apartment. Their friends' departure at midnight felt like an exodus, leaving behind an eerie emptiness. Sarah entered the kitchen, a collection of empty bottles cradled in her arms. "Hey, Kristen—I'm sorry I let it slip about your family."

"It's okay. We were with friends. But sometimes people get kind of weird when they find out."

"I get that, and I'm sorry. I should have kept my mouth shut." Sarah hesitated. "I've seen how hard you work."

Kristen embraced her friend. "Thank you. I know what the perception is of a trust-fund kid, and I guess I'm a little sensitive because here I am, someone who has been given a big leg-up in life, but I'm nothing more than an over-educated twenty-seven-year-old who works at a bookstore."

Sarah delivered a playful punch to Kristen's shoulder. "I thought you loved working there! And I didn't tell anyone you had a trust fund. My lips are sealed."

"I do love the bookstore. You know ... a bookstore clerk isn't exactly something my parents can brag about to their friends. Right?"

"Who cares! Hey, live your dream, girl." Sarah grinned. "Besides, they can always brag about your sister."

Kristen laughed. What would she do when Sarah was gone? Leah, Todd, Mike, and Michelle would still be around, but would she feel like a fifth wheel among the couples? Would the dynamic shift? "I'm going to miss you, friend. Will I see you before you leave in the morning? I work at nine."

Sarah turned off the light in the now sparkling-clean kitchen. "I'm going to miss you too. I need to leave for the airport by eight. How about we grab breakfast together at Lindy's before that. Is seven o'clock too early?"

"Not at all. I'll see you in the morning."

"Great! Goodnight."

Kristen retreated to her room and settled into bed, but sleep eluded her. In the darkness, she stared at the ceiling, contemplating Jason's earlier comment—"must be nice." Yeah, it was—sometimes. But it wasn't like what people imagined. She wasn't a spoiled rich girl. Her ten-year-old dented Jetta was just fine with her. Kristen had to admit she appreciated not having the massive student loans burdening most of her friends, but she hadn't sat idle. She had worked through most of college—not out of necessity, but because Mary's Bookshop was her sanctuary. But now, wasn't it time to move on?

The rejection letters from eight different publishing houses weighed heavily on her mind as the next step and the uncertainty of her career path loomed. Was being an editor truly her calling, or was it merely a logical progression with her degree? Living in New York with her sister sounded enticing, and Kristen loved reading books, but doubts lingered. As she rolled over and closed her eyes, she resolved that if another rejection letter arrived, law school would become her next venture.

CHAPTER THREE

Kristen shared one last embrace with Sarah as the cab idled in front of Lindy's Coffee House. Sarah opened the door, paused, and spoke, "Thank you for watering my plants while I'm gone. If you have to move before I get back, Michelle said she'd take care of them. But, selfishly, I'm hoping you'll still be here at the end of the summer."

Kristen nodded, masking the difficulty of the farewell with a light tone. "Maybe. Who knows, right?"

"Right." Sarah entered the cab, fastening her seatbelt. "Bye, Kristen. Have a great summer!"

"You too. Hey, send me a postcard every once in a while!"

"You got it!"

As the cab pulled away, Kristen glanced at her watch—five minutes after eight. It was too early for work, and the morning beckoned with its beauty. Kristen re-entered Lindy's and ordered one more coffee to go. A walk to the park seemed like the perfect way to clear her head and engage in some contemplative prayer.

Forty minutes later, Kristen glided through the bookshop's front door, a smile adorning her face as the rustic bell on the door announced her arrival. Mary's Bookshop, nestled in a corner of downtown Moscow, exuded a charm that felt like a well-worn page from Kristen's favorite novel. Its exterior, adorned with ivy-covered bricks, welcomed book lovers into a haven of literary treasures. Inside, cozy nooks scattered with worn armchairs and reading lamps invited customers to lose themselves in the magic of storytelling among the shelves upon shelves of neatly organized books, their spines forming a mosaic of colors and titles.

Lavender, the shop's resident cat, rubbed against Kristen's legs, and she greeted her with a gentle scratch. Mary Miller, the beloved owner of the bookstore and Kristen's mother figure, mentor, and friend, ascended the basement stairs with a tray of chocolate cupcakes.

"Kristen! Good morning!"

"Good morning, Mary. Those cupcakes smell amazing!"

"Don't they? It's all I can do not to eat them all myself." Mary set the tray down and enveloped Kristen in a warm hug. "Welcome back, honey. Did you have a nice visit with your family?"

Kristen stowed her purse behind the counter as Mary arranged the cupcakes. "Yes, I did, but it's good to be back."

Mary nodded, her Irish accent lending a melodic cadence to her words. She unclasped her floral print apron and began searching her pockets with uncharacteristic urgency. "Ah, yes. I'm glad. Huh. Where are my glasses?"

Before Kristen could respond, Mary reached up and touched the missing glasses perched on the top of her head. Laughing, she shook her head. "I swear, if my head weren't attached to my body, I'd lose that, too!"

"It happens to everyone." Kristen smiled. "Where would you like me to start today?"

"We got a new shipment in the back. How about you unpack those boxes and get the inventory out on the floor, and I'll work the register. If anyone wants to order coffee, though, I'll need you to take care of it. I still haven't figured out that new machine. Annabelle is coming in for her shift at one, and then I was hoping we could talk this afternoon."

The bakery case and the coffee bar, with an espresso machine, were two recent additions to the store that they were all still getting used to, but which were already drawing in new customers.

Before Kristen could ask Mary if everything was okay, the jingle of the bell drew her attention to three women entering the store. Mary moved to welcome them, and Kristen headed to the back room to retrieve the new inventory. Throughout the morning, both she and Mary kept busy. The chocolate cupcakes sold out by eleven and Kristen lost count of how many lattes she made, scolding herself for forgetting to don an apron when she spilled one on her blouse.

Since she didn't live far from the bookstore, Kristen decided to go home during her lunch break to change clothes. As she retrieved her mail, her eyes landed on an envelope bearing Doubleday's logo. Tearing it open, Kristen's heart raced as she began to peruse the letter. A moment later, she sighed and tossed it aside. Well, then ... time to apply to law school.

***

Returning to the bookshop an hour later, Kristen exchanged waves with Annabelle, who, perched at the register, sported another vibrant hair color. Today, it was bold purple, a stark contrast to the pink hue from a month ago.

"Hey, Annabelle. You okay out here on your own for a few more minutes? Mary said she had something she wanted to talk to me about in her office."

Annabelle nodded, and Kristen made her way to the back of the store. Anabelle had been working there for about six months after school and in the summer. Despite her flamboyant appearance, the girl's shy demeanor surprised those who met her. Kristen didn't know much else about the young woman other than she enjoyed her job and was both reliable and very sweet.

Mary was on the phone when Kristen poked her head in the door, but she gestured for her to come in and sit down. Pushing aside a stack of books from the only other chair in the office, Kristen paused to run her hand over a mustard-colored book on top of the pile she hadn't seen before. It was a vintage clothbound book titled *Mrs. Canfield's Cookery Book for the Modern Woman*. Kristen carefully opened the cover and leafed through the cookbook's pages, surprised to discover delightful handwritten quotes adorning the margins with meticulous penmanship. Next to a recipe for shortbread, someone had penned the Emily Dickinson poem, To Wait an Hour — is Long.

> *To wait an Hour - is long -*
> *If Love be just beyond -*
> *To wait Eternity - is short -*
> *If Love reward the end.*

After Mary bid farewell to the person on the other end of the phone line and placed the phone back on the cradle, she gestured toward the cookbook. "That one came in with a shipment of used books the other day. It seems to have quite a story to go along with it; did you see it was published in 1916? I couldn't bear to part with it and thought I'd try out a few of the recipes for our bakery case."

"Oh, that will be fun. Yes, I can see this book has been well-loved." Kristen placed the book on Mary's desk. "So, what did you want to talk about?"

Mary sighed. "My sister in Dublin had a stroke last week. She's going to be okay, but she has a long road to recovery in front of her. Alice is in the hospital right now, but once she's out, I'll need to go take care of her since she doesn't have any other family." She drummed her fingers on the desk. "I don't know what to do about the store. I know it's a lot to ask, but what would you think of taking over while I'm gone? No pressure, honey. If I need to close the shop for a while, so be it. It will still be here when I get back."

Kristen felt her heart race, and goosebumps tingled on her arms. She wanted to say yes immediately, but this was a significant decision. "Oh ... I'm sorry to hear about your sister. Um, wow. Operate the store? How long will you be gone?"

Mary leaned back in her chair, took off her glasses, and rubbed the bridge of her nose. "How long? A couple of months, probably. I'm not sure, but I know you can do it. I trust you. You love this place as much as I do; it shows. Of course, with the extra responsibilities, I'll give you a raise ...."

Mary was right. Kristen loved this store. It had been like a second home for her throughout her college years and a beloved gathering place for many others in the community. She couldn't imagine Moscow without Mary's Bookshop.

Kristen remembered what she'd prayed about in the park earlier that morning. She'd asked for direction regarding her future—and a clear sign. Was the publisher's rejection letter her sign to attend law school? Or was Mary's request for her to manage the bookstore her sign to stay at the shop a while longer? Kristen cleared her throat. "When do you need your answer?"

"I leave in three days," Mary shrugged sheepishly. I know... not a lot of time to think about it. Of course, if you already have another job lined up, I understand. I just ... I don't have anyone else to ask."

Kristen paused, closed her eyes, and took a deep breath. A quiet inner voice prompted her to say, "I'll do it."

Mary's eyes welled with tears as she grabbed Kristen's hand. "Thank you, dear. I can't tell you how much this means to me." She paused, then smiled sheepishly. "There's one more thing. I have to ask … can you also care for my cat"?"

Kristen smiled, "Of course! I'll take good care of Lavender"."

Relief washed over Mary's face, and she let out a sigh. "Oh, bless you, Kristen. Lavender is like family to me. She's got her favorite sunny spot by the window, and don't forget her evening treat of salmon-flavored kibble. And, well, she might give you a hard time about being in my office. It's her domain, you know?"

Kristen chuckled, "Noted. Lavender's comfort is a top priority. Anything else I should know?"

Mary thought for a moment. "Oh, she loves the sound of soft music. I usually play some classical tunes for her when I'm closing up shop. It seems to soothe her. And, of course, if you ever need to find her in a hurry, just shake the treat bag."

As they continued discussing the finer points of daily operations, Kristen couldn't help but feel a growing sense of responsibility and connection to the bookstore and its feline resident. The bookstore had always been a place of comfort and inspiration for her, and now, she was stepping into a role that would allow her to contribute to its continued success.

With the details of 'managing the bookstore in her absence settled, Mary leaned back in her chair, a mix of gratitude and tears in her eyes. "Kristen, you have no idea what a relief this is for me. I've been so worried about the shop, and now I can leave knowing it's in good hands. And Lavender, too."

Kristen smiled warmly, "It's my pleasure, Mary. I'll take care of everything here. You focus on your sister, and when you come back, the bookstore will be just as you left it."

As she stood up to return to the front of the store, she couldn't shake the feeling that this was more than just a temporary job opportunity.

CHAPTER FOUR

After nearly tripping over Lavender, Kristen gently scooped up the cat, offering a comforting scratch on the neck. Lavender purred and affectionately rubbed her head against Kristen's hand. The poor creature obviously missed Mary, as evidenced by a new habit of following Kristen around the store. Mary had been gone three days—enough time for Kristen to wonder if agreeing to run the bookstore might have been biting off more than she could chew. The relaxed and cozy atmosphere usually present in the shop was attributable to Mary, who was so good at her job that she made everything seem easy. It didn't come without skill and effort, as Kristen was now learning.

Kristen had a long list of questions written in her notebook, ready to ask when Mary called. She was expecting the call any minute, which could be a problem. It was Annabelle's day off, so Kristen was the sole employee in the store and six customers were currently browsing the shelves. Kristen set Lavender down behind the counter as a woman approached. "Excuse me, Miss? I'd like to order a tall nonfat vanilla latte. And do you have any more of those chocolate cupcakes you had the other day?"

"I'm sorry, we're out of the cupcakes." Kristen made a mental note to add cupcakes to her list of questions. How was she supposed to keep the pastry case stocked on top of everything else she was doing? "Would you like that latte hot or iced?"

The lady sighed, expressing her disappointment: "Hot, please. I was really looking forward to a cupcake."

While Kristen was making the latte, the phone rang. There was no choice but to let the machine get it since a line had formed at the register. Hopefully, Mary would try again later. Perspiration dampened the back of Kristen's neck, and she felt her pulse racing as a sense of overwhelm crept in. But she tried to remain outwardly calm as she called out, "I'll be with you in a moment. Sorry, it's just me today."

A warm smile, followed by a wave, was offered by the older man at the front of the line. "Take your time, dear, you're fine."

Ten minutes later, Kristen placed the newest book by Debbie Macomber in a paper bag and handed it to the woman who'd ordered the latte. She'd served everyone, and she'd kept her cool throughout. After the woman walked outside, Kristen looked around, making sure she and Lavender were the only ones left. Glancing at the clock, she noted it was five o'clock. Closing time. Kristen picked up the cat and twirled her around. "We did it!"

As soon as she turned the sign to say they were closed and locked the door, the telephone rang again. Kristen hurried to pick it up. "Mary's Bookshop, how may I help you?"

"Hello, Kristen. It's Mary. How's it going?"

Kristen smiled at the sound of Mary's voice and relaxed against the edge of the counter. "Not too bad. It was a busy day. How's your sister?"

"She's going to need a lot of time to recover, but she's home."

"A lot of time?"

"Yes, how would you feel about running the store for longer than we discussed? I'm not sure what our timeline is going to look like."

Kristen fiddled with the pen in her hand as she thought through different scenarios. "I'm open to that idea, but we need more help. Would you be open to hiring another employee?"

"Of course! I was just going to suggest that. If you say yes, dear, I want you to feel free to make decisions as if the store was your own. You have my complete trust."

By the time Kristen said goodbye, they'd come up with a plan. Once again, she'd said yes to Mary's request for help. A frisson of excitement overcame Kristen as she thought of the possibilities. Having Mary's complete trust meant the world to her. Once she hired some extra help, she would be free to implement some ideas for the store that had been rolling around her mind for some time. She wanted to start a book club, and it was definitely time to change the window display. And it would be fun to try out some new recipes for the pastry case. She picked up *Mrs. Canfield's Cookery Book* and decided to take it home with her. Perhaps she'd find some inspiration.

Kristen walked through the store, turning off the lights. Lavender was sleeping on her favorite chair in the children's section. Kristen paused. Would the cat prefer to come home with her each night? Would she be lonely by herself? Mary lived above the store, and Lavender had always had the freedom to come and go as she pleased between the two spaces. Since she seemed content for now, Kristen decided to leave her there. "See you in the morning, kitty."

***

Several days later, after Kristen's call with Mary, Josh Brooks arrived at the bookstore five minutes ahead of schedule for his three o'clock interview, punctuality that immediately set him apart from the previous candidate, who had sauntered in fifteen minutes late in a disheveled ensemble. Kristen couldn't help but think that Josh was already the frontrunner for the job.

As Kristen examined Josh's application, a graduate student seeking part-time work with retail experience, she noticed Annabelle listed as a reference. Her gaze then shifted toward the man before her. A sense of familiarity crossed her mind. Did they share a class? Josh appeared to be someone who embraced the outdoors, evident in his sun-bleached hair, tan skin, and athletic build. He wore khakis with a neatly ironed plaid button-down shirt, and his dark-rimmed glasses framed deep brown eyes that sparkled with kindness.

Kristen cleared her throat, feeling a flutter of nervousness during only her second interview. "So, how do you know Annabelle, Josh?"

"Annabelle is my cousin. She told me you could use some extra help here. I've worked retail before, I read a lot, and enjoy talking about books, so I think I might be a good fit for the job."

"Ah, yes. I see you're a student. What are you studying?"

"Creative writing." Josh paused, his face lighting up with recognition. "Hey, were you in Ted Filson's theater and film class last fall? You look familiar."

"I was in that class! And I thought I recognized you too. Yeah, that was a fun class." Kristen relaxed, settling back in her chair. "Are you available to work weekends?"

Josh nodded. "Yes, and I can start right away."

They continued chatting for a few more minutes as Kristen restrained an impulse to hire him immediately. She decided to speak to Annabelle first to ensure Josh wasn't too good to be true. "Well, thank you for coming in. I'll be in touch and let you know what we decide."

Josh stood, offered a handshake, and smiled. His smile was adorable. Kristen guessed it charmed many girls, but she wouldn't let it charm her. If she were going to be his boss, professionalism would need to be the name of the game.

CHAPTER FIVE

Mrs. Canfield's scone recipe looked simple enough, though she'd had to guess at details like oven temperature and baking time. The cookbook only gave vague directions, such as *place in hot oven until done.* Kristen was mixing another batch when her phone rang. The sticky dough clung to her hands as she tried to wipe them clean on a towel before picking up the phone. "Hello?"

"Hey, Kristen, how are you?" Her mother's chipper voice asked.

Kristen slid a tray into the oven. "Hey, Mom, I'm good ... just doing some baking. I've been meaning to call you. I have some news."

"You got a job?"

"Well ... actually," Kristen drew in a deep breath. "My boss at the bookstore had a family emergency and 'I've agreed to run the store for a few months."

An awkward silence ensued before her mom responded. "That's very kind of you, honey. But what happens if you get a job offer from one of the publishing companies in the meantime?"

"Doubleday rejected me." Kristen yanked a loose string from the towel she was holding. "I don't think it's going to happen ... and I don't want to go to law school." She held her breath, awaiting her mother's reaction.

"Okay, well then, how's it going running the store?"

"Not bad. I'm exhausted, but I just hired someone to help out, so it should get better."

Kristen relaxed, feeling relief wash over her as she realized her mom was not going to give her a hard time about her decision. They talked for a while longer until Kristen caught a whiff of something burning.

"Oh! I forgot the scones!"

Kristen grabbed a hot pad and pulled the charred remains out of the oven. They weren't going to be salvageable.

"You're making scones?"

"Yes, I found this old cookbook at the store, and I thought the scones might be good to sell with the coffee."

"Oh, honey ... you're baking them in your apartment and selling them at the shop? You have a permit, right?"

"Ugh. I don't know, actually. Don't worry; I'm not planning on selling these ones. They're burnt and going straight into the garbage. I assume Mary took care of all the permits. She recently brought in an espresso machine and started selling baked goods. They've been a hit with the customers."

Even as Kristen said the words, a cloud of doubt entered her mind. Did Mary have a permit to sell food in the shop?

"I only ask because I don't want you to get into trouble. I don't know about the rules in Idaho, but here in Washington, you can get fined for baking and selling goods from your home. Ask me how I know."

Kristen didn't need to ask because she remembered. Years ago, her mother, former bake sale queen, had been slapped with a thousand-dollar fine after selling homemade cupcakes for the high school P.T.A. The penalty was eventually dropped, but not without a lot of drama, and not until the story was splashed around the local press. Kristen had always suspected there was more to the story. That incident likely resulted from a tip-off connected to the ongoing scramble for higher rank in the pecking order between her friends' mothers throughout her school years. Her mother, Betsy Borstad, P.T.A. president, was a target of jealous rivals.

"Oh, I remember." Kristen plopped into an easy chair. "I'll double-check with Mary on the permit next time I talk to her."

It was late when Kristen said goodbye to her mother and put down the phone. Her body felt less tense than before the call, but now a pang of regret niggled at the back of her mind. In an effort to sound confident about her decision, she'd been less than forthright with her mother about how overwhelmed she really was. The truth was, she had some doubts. Was running Mary's bookstore really what God wanted her to do?

Kristen was too tired to clean up the mess in the kitchen. It could wait until morning. Instead, she plopped onto the couch, opened *Mrs. Canfield's Cookery Book*, and studied the notes in the margins in an attempt to discover the book's secrets. It had obviously been loved throughout its many years. From the different handwriting styles in the margins, Kristen surmised that it had been passed around a fair amount.

The book belonged to Mary, but it felt like a special privilege to have it in her possession. Kristen decided she'd give the scones another attempt tomorrow if she had time. She needed a day off. How many days had it been that she'd worked in a row? Ten? Running a bookstore wasn't easy.

Tomorrow would be Josh's first day at the shop. Would he quickly pick up on everything he needed to learn? He seemed like a smart guy, and he was personable and charming—and yes, he was cute. The customers would love him. Kristen hoped her first big decision as guardian over Mary's store was the right one, but she had a positive feeling about Josh and was grateful that the extra help would give her some much-needed breathing room.

Before she closed the cookbook, Kristen's eyes rested on a handwritten note next to the recipe for scones. Her favorite Bible verse,

"Our soul waits for the Lord; He is our help and our shield. -Psalm 33:20."

Next to the verse, in different handwriting, someone had handwritten a single word in beautiful calligraphy: serenity. What did that word, *serenity,* or that verse have to do with scones? Kristen slowly ran her finger over the letters as she pondered the meaning. It's a beautiful word, she thought— and it's what I want.

***

Kristen cherished the early morning hours spent alone in the bookstore before it officially opened. The tranquility of this time, with only Lavender for company, was heightened by the sunlight streaming through the front windows, creating enchanting shadows on the polished wood floors as she lifted the blinds. As the coffee pot percolated, Kristen powered up the computer at the front counter before descending to the basement office, where she pulled out the company checkbook to tackle invoices before Josh's arrival.

An hour later, Kristen sealed the last envelope of outgoing mail with a sense of accomplishment. With the office work completed, she began sifting through Mary's filing cabinet for a county health department permit. The lack of any permit in sight intensified her concern. Leaning back in her chair, she decided to simplify the coffee bar offerings until she could confirm their legality. Lavender hopped onto her lap, and as Kristen caressed the cat's soft fur, she whispered, "You'll need to keep yourself on the down low; the health department might not appreciate your presence here."

Venturing upstairs, the sound of knocking reached Kristen's ears—*Josh!* She felt a twinge of guilt for losing track of time and opened the door with an apologetic smile. "Josh, I'm so sorry! I hope you weren't waiting long. I was in the basement, and I didn't hear you. Come on in. And good morning!"

Josh, ever good-natured, shrugged off any inconvenience. "Good morning. And hey, no worries. How are you?"

"I'm glad you're here, that's how I am. I hope you're ready to jump right in. Tuesday mornings can get kind of busy around here." Kristen glanced at her watch and decided to turn the door sign to "open." "Come with me. I'll show you where you can put your stuff, and then give you a tour of the rest of the store."

When Kristen introduced Josh to Lavender, who had been napping in the front display window, she observed the immediate connection between them. Josh's affinity for cats added another point in his favor. As Kristen led him through each section of the store, a sense of pride swelled within her. 'Even though it wasn't her store, she had invested significant time and effort in each section, imprinting her touch on the various displays. Josh's enthusiasm and genuine interest in the details felt like validation. Hiring him seemed like an excellent decision.

Soon, Annabelle joined them, and the store buzzed with customers. With Josh confidently handling the front counter and Annabelle assigned to the coffee bar, Kristen left for lunch. Seated at a booth in the deli across the street, Kristen munched on a turkey sandwich and began to consider the realm of possibilities for the store. Grabbing a napkin and pen, she initiated a list with "Start a book club" at the top of her list.

CHAPTER SIX

Josh, who'd been working at the shop a week already, was proving to be a true godsend. He'd quickly picked up everything he needed to know, and, as expected, the customers loved him. Her new employee had been handling everything out front that morning. It helped, of course, that he didn't have to make lattes and run the register simultaneously. That was too much for one person to do.

After Kristen learned they'd been operating without a permit, she'd reluctantly shut down the coffee bar. It was only temporary, but there had been an immediate outcry from their regulars. If all went well today, they'd be happy. If not, those customers would soon find another place to go for their morning treats. It was important that she not lose their business.

Kristen wanted to make Mary happy and increase—not decrease—sales while she was in Ireland. Not that Mary had ever placed any pressure on her. It was just the opposite, really. In their last phone conversation, her boss had once again assured Kristen that there would be no hard feelings if it were necessary to shut down the shop temporarily so that Kristen could accept a job in the publishing industry. But Kristen knew that wouldn't happen. Besides, Annabelle and Josh relied on their weekly paychecks.

The rainy day lull in business allowed Kristen some extra time in the small, tucked-away kitchen in the basement to go over her list and survey the space one more time before the inspector arrived. Everything was sparkling clean and ready to go. Kristen put a chocolate chip scone on a plate, flipped off the light switch, and went upstairs. She found Josh by the front register. "Here, try this," she said, passing him the plate. "See if you like it." He took a bite of the scone, and, as she'd hoped, a look of delight spread across his face. '

"Oh, wow! These are really good!"

"Thanks! I'm glad you like them. Hopefully, the inspector 'will like them, too. He'll be here at three o'clock, and if all goes well, our little coffee counter will be fully back in business soon." "Kristen moved to the computer. "Everything we sell has to be labeled, so that's what I'm going to do now … package and label the scones."

She'd designed cute labels with a logo featuring a simple line drawing of an old-fashioned, grandmotherly-type lady. The tags said "Mrs. Canfield's Chocolate-Chip Scones" and listed all the ingredients and allergens as required.

She'd expand their line of baked offerings later, but for now, all she had to do was print the labels off. Unfortunately, the printer wasn't responding. Kristen huffed, "What, now?"

Josh grinned, "Do you want some help?" As he moved closer, the fresh scent of lemony soap wafted toward Kristen.

"Sure. I can never seem to get this printer to work."

After Josh clicked a few buttons on the computer, the printer came to life, and Kristen breathed a sigh of relief.

Josh picked up the printed labels and then exclaimed, "Hey, these are fantastic!' Who is Mrs. Canfield?"

"She was the author of an old cookbook that I came across the other day. I got the recipe from her, so it felt right to give her credit. But the way I drew her here, she looks a little like Mary, the owner of this store." Kristen laughed.

The rest of the afternoon went by peacefully enough as the rain continued. Even though it was summer, the day was dark and cool, so Kristen turned on the gas fireplace in the reading nook, which added a cozy atmosphere to the store. Josh rushed off to one of his 'classes when his shift ended at two, and soon after, one of their regulars, Harold Reese, came in, looking for the newest Michael Crichton novel and some conversation.

When Annabelle arrived, Kristen was surprised to notice it was already three o'clock. As she greeted Annabelle, a middle-aged man with a crewcut, a clipboard, and a short-sleeved dress shirt came through the front door. He propped his umbrella against the front counter and looked around. "You must be Kristen Borstad?" Kristen nodded, and he held out his hand. "Stan Smith. County Health Department."

Kristen shook his hand. "Nice to meet you; thank you for coming. I'll show you the kitchen."

Guiding Stan through the store, Kristen prayed Lavender wouldn't decide to grace them with her presence. Opening the door to the kitchen, she flipped on the light switch and gasped. The entire floor was covered in at least an inch of water and more was bubbling up from a drain under the sink. Kristen's heart sank. She glanced at the inspector, who frowned and shook his head.

Stan sighed, "Sorry, I can't issue you a permit. You're going to have to call a plumber. You can try again one more time after this unfortunate situation is rectified, but that will be your last chance."

***

A vice seemed to tighten around Kristen's head as she hung up the phone and scratched out a note on the first piece of paper. she could find. A plumber named Darrell was on his way, but it would cost extra for the emergency service call—$800 minimum. She pondered her options; paying extra for emergency service seemed inevitable. At least the flooding was contained to the kitchen area, but still, she dreaded telling Mary the bad news. She'd have to ask if this problem was covered by insurance.

While she waited for Darrell to arrive, she decided to catch up on some emails. Annabelle had everything under control at the front of the store, and anyhow, Kristen was too frazzled to face any customers at the moment.

An audible gasp escaped her as she opened the first email. She'd interviewed with Simon and Schuster over two months ago but had given up on ever hearing back. Now, they wanted to talk to her about an offer. A smile tugged at Kristen's lips. A job offer from Simon and Schuster! But was this what she truly wanted? Was leaving the right thing to do? Kristen leaned back in her chair and took a deep breath. She wasn't sure how long she sat there, staring into space, weighing her options.

A knock on the open door interrupted her train of thought, bringing her back to the present. "The plumber is here," Annabelle said. I showed him down to the kitchen."

Gratitude filled Kristen's voice. 'Thank you, Annabelle." She glanced at the clock on the wall. "It's almost six o'clock. You can close up and go home."

When Kristen walked into the kitchen, she was relieved to see that most of the water had gone back down the drain. But why had it happened? And how long would this delay the permit?

Darrell kicked his toe against the drain. "It's probably a problem with roots in the pipes. That happens in these older buildings. I'll send a snake down there to check it out."

Noticing the look on Kristen's face, Darrell chuckled. "It's not a real snake; it's a tool. 'I'll get this taken care of tomorrow morning. Don't worry; your kitchen should be usable again by the end of the week."

Darrell packed up his things and soon left. A sigh of relief escaped Kristen as she proceeded to lock up the store. It had been a long day. In the quiet of the evening, Kristen whispered, "Father God, guide me, reveal Your will for my life. What should I do?"

CHAPTER SEVEN

Three days later, Kristen luxuriated in the stillness of her soft bed and the ability to sleep a little longer than usual since the store didn't open until noon on Sundays. She was grateful for the extra time, as she hadn't been able to fall asleep until the early morning hours. The clock on the nightstand showed it was eight o'clock. If she got up now, she could still attend the early service at church before she went to work. She pushed the covers aside and swung her legs over the edge of the bed.

With the kitchen drain issue resolved, as Darrell promised, her only pressing concern was whether to take the job in New York. She needed to give them her answer by tomorrow.

'Lavender rubbed against Kristen's legs and purred. 'With the recent basement flooding, Kristen had decided to start taking the animal back and forth between the shop and the apartment. It was an arrangement that seemed to suit both of them, but now posed another problem. Who would care for the poor creature if she moved before Mary returned? "Hey, sweetie. You hungry?"

Kristen, feeling a chill, grabbed her robe and wrapped it around her before heading toward the kitchen to find some breakfast for both of them. As the coffee brewed, Kristen sorted through a stack of mail on the counter. She stuck the postcard she recently got from Sarah to the fridge with a magnet. It was a picture of Bondi Beach. The short message assured her that her roommate was having a great time in

Australia and mentioned she'd met some fun people to hang out with at the hostel. Kristen wished she could be with her friend right now. It would be comforting to have someone to talk to, someone who could offer her valuable advice. She had prayed and asked God for guidance, but it seemed that He was remaining silent for now. Maybe she'd hear from Him at church today.

Thirty minutes later, Kristen pulled into the parking lot at Grace Chapel as Leah and Todd were getting out of their car.

Leah rushed toward her with a giant coffee tumbler in hand. "Kristen! It's been ages! How have you been? Want to join us this morning?"

Kristen smiled. "Sure, thanks. I'm good, but I've missed seeing you around! We need to get together for dinner again soon."

Todd caught up with them. "Hey, how's it going?"

"Busy! My boss, Mary, went to Ireland to help her sister, and I've been running the bookshop. How've you been?"

"Oh, wow ... cool. I'm taking a couple of classes this summer, but it's been pretty chill." They were almost to the entrance. "We're going to get some brunch at The Pancake House afterward. Want to come?"

She would have to watch the time carefully, but hanging out with friends for a bit would feel good. "Yeah, I'd like that."

"Great! We're going to invite a bunch of people, so feel free to include anyone you think of."

Kristen nodded, then followed her friends to their seats. Grace Chapel was a small but warm-hearted faith community that met in a white clapboard building with a classic steeple and more than one hundred years of history. It was one of the original buildings on Main Street, and the congregations comprised a mixture of students and families, along with a few silver-headed elders. From the first time she'd visited eight years ago—right after moving to Moscow—until now, it had remained a source of comfort and a place where she'd learned and grown as a Christian.

The congregation was already singing, "Be Thou My Vision." It was one of her favorite hymns. Right away, she spotted Josh across the aisle, two rows up. *He goes to church here? Huh.* She'd never seen him there before.

As the minister preached from a passage in Philippians, Kristen's thoughts drifted to the uncertainties about her future. If she turned down the job with the publishing company, would she be throwing away the best opportunity she'd ever get to really make something of herself?

But what about the bookstore? She'd been confident that God had led her to 'accept Mary's request. Had she been wrong? Kristen refocused her attention on the words being spoken.

"And I am sure of this, that he who began a good work in you will bring it to completion at the day of Jesus Christ. Philippians 1:6"

Kristen glanced at her watch after the service ended. She wouldn't have much time to eat brunch with her friends. Should she bail and go straight to the store instead? Before she could make a decision, Josh came over.

"Hey, Todd, hey Kristen. How's it going?"

Huh. Does Josh already know Todd? "Hi, Josh. Good. How long have you been coming here?"

"Just a couple of weeks, but I think I'm going to stick around."

Kristen nodded. She'd been so busy with the store she'd missed the last few weeks. "Well, good to see you. And you know Todd?"

Todd smiled and held out his hand toward Josh. "Yeah, we met last week. Hey, Josh, we're going to the Pancake House. Want to come?"

"Sure. Thanks!" He looked at Kristen. "You coming, too?"

"Uh ... yeah." Pancakes did sound good. "But I won't be able to stay long. I have to get to work soon."

At the restaurant, Kristen found a big group of people from church seated at a long table in the back room. *Todd and Leah sure organized this crowd quickly!* There was only one chair left; the one next to Josh.

***

On Monday, Kristen rushed home for lunch, eager for her scheduled call with Sally Tompkins, the hiring manager at Simon and Schuster. While waiting for the phone to ring, she hurriedly went to the fridge, dished up some leftover chicken pot pie, and stuck it in the microwave.

The chicken pot pie was another successful recipe she'd recently made from *Mrs. Canfield's Cookery Book for the Modern Woman.* Considering that it wasn't actually her book to keep and because the cookbook was one-of-a-kind, Kristen started copying some of her favorite recipes into a cloth-covered notebook. In the spirit of the original, she also added verses, quotes, and illustrations around the margins.

The phone rang, interrupting her attempt to savor the first bite of her reheated lunch. Kristen glanced at the caller' ID. This was it. She cleared her throat and took a deep breath before picking it up. "Hello. This is Kristen."

The woman's voice on the other end—straightforward and businesslike—left no room for ambiguity. "Kristen, this is Sally Tompkins from Simon and Schuster. How are you today?" She didn't wait for an answer. "I assume you've looked over our offer, and I'm calling to arrange your next steps."

Next steps. Kristen pondered the irreversible nature of her upcoming words, realizing there would be no retreat from the path she was about to choose.

While listening to Josh at brunch yesterday, she was struck by his passion and excitement when he talked about the novel he was working on. She'd wondered, *what is it that ignites a similar flame in me?* Upon further reflection, 'Kristen realized her passion wasn't in becoming an editor; it was rooted in the meaningful work she was currently doing at the bookstore.

"Sally, thank you for calling, and yes, I've reviewed the offer. I appreciate your time and your interest, but I must decline. It's a good offer, but I've had something else come up."

After Kristen hung up the phone, she lowered herself onto the floor and sat silently.

Oh, God. I believe I made the right choice, but I'm going to need every ounce of strength and guidance You can offer me.

CHAPTER EIGHT

Kristen busied herself for the first book club meeting, setting out plates, napkins, lemon bars, and coffee. How many people would show up? What if nobody came? It was hard to know what to expect, but she was feeling cautiously optimistic based on the positive responses she'd received from several customers. Mary had generously offered the use of her apartment upstairs after Kristen had informed her of the plan to host a book club at the store.

Mary's living area was bathed in natural light, creating an airy space with a bird's-eye view of Main Street. It was decorated with an eclectic mix of English floral upholstered furniture and cheerful landscape art—all painted by Mary. The floor-to-ceiling shelves along one wall housed just part of Mary's extensive personal library. The rest of the books were stacked in numerous towers. The room was hushed and snug, providing comfortable seating for five or six, creating the perfect atmosphere for engaging in bookish conversations.

After a final glance around the room, Kristen was satisfied. There was enough time to run downstairs before the group arrived and make sure Josh had everything he needed to run the shop independently over the next couple of hours.

He was finishing up a phone call when Kristen approached the front counter. After hanging up, he turned his attention toward her. "Ugh, health inspector. Last-minute cancellation. He wants to swing by this afternoon for a kitchen recheck. Does that work for you?

It was good news—sort of. If all went well, Kristen could reopen the coffee bar sooner than expected. But what about the book club? Josh spoke again, interrupting her thoughts. "I can show him around. It will be okay."

"Okay. If the store is busy when he gets here, just come get me. Thank you!"

"No problem," Josh replied, a reassuring smile on his face.

"Oh, and we should probably keep Lavender out of the way. I'll take her upstairs with me."

Just then, two middle-aged women Kristen recognized as regular customers came through the front door. Kristen smiled and greeted them.

"Hi, Heidi. Hi, Matilda. '"

Heidi smiled in return. "Hi, Kristen. We're here for the book club."

"Oh, great! I'm glad you're here. Follow me!"

Kristen led the women upstairs. Soon, three more women joined them: Irene, Julie, and Ruby. The presence of these women buoyed Kristen's spirit. They all seemed enthusiastic to be there, and she was happy she'd followed through on her desire to start a book club. "Help yourself to some lemon bars, ladies, and then we'll get started."

Ruby, a petite silver-haired woman wearing bold, red-framed glasses, sat beside Kristen. "Oh, wow, honey—these lemon bars are divine."

"Thank you. I've been trying out some recipes from an antique cookbook that found its way to this store, *Mrs. Canfield's Cookery Book for the Modern Woman*. It's been a lot of fun."

Irene held out her cup of coffee as if she were about to give a toast. "Well, keep it up. Ruby is right. These are amazing. And may I say, thank you ... not just for the lemon bars, but for organizing this book club."

Kristen felt her cheeks warm as all eyes turned to her. The chatter in the room had quieted. "How about we kick things off with some introductions?"

An hour later, after the meeting was over, Kristen said goodbye to her new friends and went downstairs to relieve Josh and let him go to lunch. "How'd it go?"

Josh was reshelving some books in the children's area. There were dry Cheerios everywhere as if they'd been thrown like confetti. He shook his head and rolled his eyes. "Why do some parents think just letting their kids run wild is okay?"

Kristen commiserated. "I know, right? This doesn't look so bad, though. I've seen it much worse. But, what about the inspection? Did he already come?"

Josh reached for the broom and began sweeping. "Yes, he was here. Lavender came into the kitchen and followed him around. I'm sorry, I didn't see her until it was too late."

Oh, no. I forgot to take the cat upstairs with me! Kristen held her breath, waiting for the bad news. Then Josh reached into his pocket and held out a slip of paper. "But he must have been in a good mood because he pretended not to notice. This is our permit!"

Overwhelmed with joy, Kristen forgot herself and impulsively hugged Josh in her excitement.

***

The Applebee's parking lot was crowded, making it a challenge for Kristen to find a spot. She looped around the building a third time. Annabelle and Josh were probably already inside waiting for her.

That afternoon, before Josh left for his class, Annabelle suggested they get together after work to celebrate the triumphant reopening of the coffee bar. Everyone happily agreed. The enthusiasm of Kristen's co-workers mirrored her own and served as a reminder that she wasn't alone when it came to the store. She had a great team behind her.

In front of Kristen, a gray Honda's reverse lights caught her attention. Perfect; a spot right in front. As she waited for the car to back up, she got a text from Annabelle.

"Sorry, I won't be able to make it. I have to take my little brother to soccer practice tonight."

Huh, Kristen thought, her excitement deflating. Would dinner with just Josh be awkward? Kristen pulled into the parking space and turned off the car. She could see him sitting alone in a booth by the window. *It's just dinner. Quit overthinking.*

Going inside the dimly lit restaurant, Kristen waved as she walked toward Josh, thankful he was already there and she could avoid the long wait with the crowd at the door.

"Hey, thanks for getting us a table." Kristen scooted into the seat across from him. "Your cousin just texted me. She's not going to make it ... something about needing to take her brother to soccer practice."

Josh raised an eyebrow. "Oh? That's weird. Sam usually rides his bike to soccer practice."

Kristen picked up a menu and shielded her face, hoping to conceal the rush of thoughts she knew were written all over her face. It was all too clear now; Annabelle was playing matchmaker.

Josh absentmindedly played with his straw. "How was the rest of the day at the store?"

Kristen lowered her menu, "It was good. Busy as usual."

They looked back at their menus, but Kristen couldn't concentrate on the food options. As much as she told herself she should remain professional, she wanted to get to know the man sitting across from her better.

"How's everything with you?" she asked, trying to sound casual.

"It's been okay." He shrugged. "Just trying to keep up with everything."

Kristen knew that Josh was going through a tough time. Annabelle told her he'd recently broken up with his longtime girlfriend and was trying to move on.

"Is everything okay?"

Josh looked up at her and smiled weakly. "Yeah, I'm fine … I've just been dealing with some relationship drama. Thanks for asking. Working at the store has been a good distraction."

They ordered their food, and as they continued to talk, Kristen couldn't help but feel drawn to Josh. For almost a month, she had been trying to ignore her attraction toward him, but instead, it was growing.

Wrapping up their meal, Josh caught Kristen off guard. "Kristen, I know we work together, but I was wondering if you'd like to go out with me sometime?"

"I would love that."

Did she really just say that? But there was no remorse. She had been suppressing her feelings for too long, and she was glad that maybe Josh felt the same way.

As they walked out of Applebee's, a spark of excitement flickered within Kristen, hinting at the potential for a romantic connection with Josh. She knew it could complicate things at work, but she was willing to take that risk.

CHAPTER NINE

Early summer sunlight streamed through Kristen's curtains, allowing her to ease into wakefulness. It was Wednesday, which meant her sister would be calling any minute. Kristen hummed a soft tune as she ground some coffee beans, the aroma quickly filling the kitchen. Over the last few weeks, she and Amy had finally worked out a routine to keep in touch despite the time difference between New York and Idaho. They'd settled on Wednesday mornings during Amy's 10 a.m. morning break, which was seven a.m. Kristen's time. Getting up early gave her a head start on her days before she went into the shop, so she didn't mind.

Taking her coffee and the cordless phone outside, Kristen settled into a deck chair on the balcony. It was already warm outside. The birds chattered animatedly, their melodies blending with the distant hum of awakening city life. Lavender jumped onto Kristen's lap just as the phone rang.

"Good morning!" Amy's voice was cheerful.

Kristen propped her feet up on the balcony's ledge. 'Hey, how's it going?"

"Did you hear about Phoebe?"

Phoebe, the family's beloved German Shepherd, was old and always going to the vet for one reason or another. Kristen's pulse quickened. *Please, no bad news.* "No ...."

"Mom put her on some kind of cottage cheese diet."

Exhale. "Oh, don't scare me like that!"

"Sorry, Kristen." Amy laughed, "So what's new with you? When are you going to join me here in New York?"

"I think I'm going to be at the bookstore until October, at least. We finally got our permit to sell bakery items for the coffee bar, and I've been having fun experimenting with different recipes from this old cookbook I found in the shop."

"So you're switching from the book industry to being a baker?"

Kristen laughed. "Who knows; maybe I can combine the two. So, how'd your date go the other night?"

"We went to a great little Greek restaurant. The food was fantastic, but the guy was boring. He seemed to be really impressed with himself. How about you? Are you getting any social life outside of the store?"

"Well, did I tell you about the new guy I hired at the bookstore?"

"No, you didn't." Amy's tone held a note of wariness. "Tell me."

"I know, I know ... it's stupid. But I'm not going to be his boss forever. Mary will come back eventually, remember?"

"Just be careful."

"I will. I promise."

Kristen decided not to share about the Monday night dinner at Applebee's. Not yet. She wasn't even sure what it meant—Josh had asked her if she wanted to go out sometime, but they had yet to make any plans. It was still ... hypothetical. Did he really mean it?

"Hey, I'm almost to my stop. I've gotta go. Love you!"

"Love you too. Have a great day!"

Kristen put the phone down with a sigh, absorbing the weight of her sister's caution. Amy's words of warning were valid. Josh was a great employee, and she didn't want to do anything to jeopardize what they already had going— a fun and casually flirtatious working relationship. But they shared so much in common, and she loved how he looked at her. He made her feel special and made her laugh. She smiled, just thinking about him.

Lavender jumped off Kristen's lap. "All right, kitty. You're right. It's time to get to work."

***

Kristen was at the bookshop by eight thirty, ready to bake a fresh batch of scones before the shop opened. Yesterday morning, the first day of reopening the coffee bar, she'd made two dozen chocolate chip scones and was pleasantly surprised when they sold out by ten. Today, she'd double the recipe and hope for a repeat performance.

She walked into the small basement kitchen and began gathering the ingredients she would need for the scones; flour, butter, sugar, baking powder, salt, chocolate chips, and milk. She set to work, preheating the oven and measuring out the ingredients.

The sound of the mixer filled the room as Kristen blended the flour and butter until the mixture resembled coarse sand. She then added the sugar and baking powder, followed by the milk, and stirred the mixture until it formed a soft dough.

Kristen's heart swelled with joy—a warm, effervescent feeling—as she anticipated the delight the delectable treats would bring to the customers. She expertly shaped the dough into triangular scones, placed them on baking trays, and slid them into the oven.

Soon, the kitchen was enveloped in the comforting embrace of a warm, buttery aroma, teasing Kristen's senses as the scones baked to golden perfection. At the sound of the timer, Kristen retrieved the scones from the oven with the utmost care and placed them gently on the wire rack to cool.

A satisfied smile played on Kristen's lips as she cleaned up the kitchen. With a sweet sense of accomplishment, she brought them upstairs, placing them in the pastry case.

Josh would be in soon. She was going to train him on the espresso machine today. While she waited, she checked the community bulletin board near the front of the store. A new flyer advertising a music festival in the park caught her attention. Reggae Cowboys was performing on Friday night. It sounded like fun. Ordinarily, she would have asked Sarah to go with her, but Sarah wouldn't be back from Australia for another month. Who else might want to go? The answer came to Kristen two hours later when Josh stood in front of the bulletin board, reading the same flyer. "Reggae Cowboys ... I saw them perform a couple of years ago. It was a good concert."

Kristen, who'd been cleaning the windows, put down the Windex and blurted out, "Do you want to go to the concert with me?" Her voice carried a tinge of excitement and vulnerability.

CHAPTER TEN

When Friday night finally arrived, Kristen spent extra time getting ready, picking out the perfect outfit, and doing her hair just right. She'd finally settled on a long Bohemian-style floral print sundress with a distressed jean jacket and platform sandals.

A fluttering anticipation gripped Kristen's chest at the knock on her front door. Seven o'clock, and there was Josh, punctual as promised. The nature of their outing lingered in ambiguity. Had this evolved into a date? The details remained shrouded, amplified by her initiation of the invitation.

Josh maneuvered his Subaru through the streets toward the park, and with each inadvertent brush of his arm against hers, Kristen's stomach fluttered with a mix of nerves and excitement. When they arrived, the atmosphere was electric. The music was loud, and the crowd was lively. Kristen smiled as Josh took her hand and led her through the crowd toward the stage.

Seated on a blanket, they savored chocolate-covered strawberries procured from a nearby food truck. Josh, ever-prepared, pulled a can of Pepsi from his backpack and extended it to Kristen. Shouting above the music, he asked, "Is this okay? Do you have everything you need?"

Kristen grinned and replied, "Yes, this is perfect. Thank you!"

Any further conversation was practically impossible, and they relaxed without the conversation pressure that's typical on first dates—if this was, in fact, a first date. Kristen was impressed by how well Josh knew the songs. Soon, they were caught up in the festive mood, singing and dancing together.

As the night unfolded, Kristen discovered herself drawn to Josh with every passing moment. His humor, charm, and effortless company made her feel as though they had known each other for years instead of just a few weeks.

The music began to wane, and a cozy atmosphere enveloped them when, unexpectedly, a rainstorm swept over the park. Everyone quickly packed up their blankets and rushed for cover. Kristen and Josh huddled together under a tree, unsuccessfully trying to stay dry.

Despite being soaked, Kristen didn't want the night to end. But as the rain continued to fall and the band left the stage, they both decided it was time to leave. They hurried back to Josh's car, soaking wet but laughing as they splashed through the puddles.

Thoughts of Josh lingered in Kristen's mind long after he dropped her off at home. Disappointment had settled in when he departed without a kiss. It was his turn to make the first move—if that was what he wanted. Did he not share the same attraction she felt for him? Tossing and turning for what felt like an eternity, she eventually succumbed to sleep, the question lingering in her thoughts.

***

The next morning, the shop was so busy Kristen didn't have time to say much more than a rushed hello to Josh as they each took their stations. She hadn't left her place by the cash register all morning, and Josh had remained on the other side of the store, cranking out the lattes. At noon, when at last there was a lull, Kristen wandered over to the coffee bar.

"Quite a whirlwind, huh? Running low on any supplies? I can dash downstairs for more milk."

"Soy milk's dwindling, and the last scone found a happy owner. Might need to double up your recipe again." He stopped what he was doing and focused on Kristen. "Fancy a cup of coffee?"

"Oh, yes, please. Just an Americano for me, if you don't mind. Thanks a bunch."

Josh filled a mug with hot water, added a shot of espresso, and handed it to Kristen. His fingers grazed hers as she took it, making her wish they had more time alone.

She took a sip of coffee and glanced around the store. The morning rush had left the place in a bit of disarray, with empty cups and used napkins strewn across the tables. The bakery counter was her labor of love, with long hours and even longer nights spent getting it ready, but it was paying off. This morning's email from Mary, a response to the latest sales figures, was an enthusiastic validation that Kristen's efforts were appreciated, not just by the customers but also by her boss. It felt good.

As she stood there, lost in her thoughts, a group of sorority girls walked in. Kristen quickly jumped up, eager to greet them and show them the hospitality that made Mary's Bookshop so popular. She welcomed them with a warm smile and quickly got to work, taking their orders and chatting with them.

As the afternoon wore on, Kristen and Josh found themselves busier than ever, with a constant stream of customers pouring in. She didn't even have a chance to take a lunch break.

At the end of the day, as the last customers filed out and the shop grew quiet, Kristen collapsed into a chair beside Josh, exhausted but happy. Looking around at the cozy, inviting space, she knew this was where she belonged—right here, at Mary's Bookshop.

"Annabelle's joining us tomorrow, so things should ease up."

"Josh, am I overloading you with hours? I know you're juggling a full class load. How's school treating you?"

"No, I'm good. The extra hours are doing wonders for the old checking account. I'll give you a heads up if it becomes too much. Writing has been easy lately ... maybe working here is the reason I've been feeling inspired. I wrote two thousand words last night after I dropped you off after the concert." Josh flashed a crooked smile. "Maybe you're my muse."

Kristen felt her face warm. "What's your book about?"

"It's a sci-fi novel, set on Earth, a hundred years from now..."

"Is it dystopian? Or did we find a way to fix our problems? Tell me more."

"First, dinner and then I spill the beans. You skipped lunch today; you must be starving. Pizza?"

"Sounds perfect."

Undeniable sparks flickered between them, causing Kristen to stand and start the process of locking up. Though uncertain if this would evolve beyond a summer flirtation, she was eager to find out.

CHAPTER ELEVEN

On Monday morning, Kristen hummed to herself as she opened the store and prepared for the new preschool story hour. The children's section was in a cheery little room conveniently adjacent to the coffee bar so the parents or caretakers could order lattes and pastries while they waited. Annabelle had volunteered to read, and Kristen had baked dozens of sugar cookies with pink frosting and rainbow sprinkles for the little ones.

Kristen surveyed the space, assessing what still needed to be done before they arrived. The familiar mustard-colored cookbook she'd been perusing earlier still sat on a low windowsill. Quickly, she picked it up, grateful she'd found the antique book before the children did.

When she'd first picked up *Mrs. Canfield's Cookery Book* in Mary's office earlier that summer, she never would have guessed how special it would become to her. It seemed as if she referred to it almost daily, not only for the recipes but also for the words of encouragement and wisdom she found amongst the pages. Next to the recipe for the sugar çookies, someone had scrawled a verse in the margins, *Proverbs 27:9, "A sweet friendship refreshes the soul."*

Kristen smiled as she read the words. In her time working at Mary's Bookshop, she'd found some sweet friendships along the way. She had the best co-workers and customers, and baking treats was one way of showing love for them.

Annabelle sailed through the front door five minutes before the story hour wearing denim overalls and glittery Converse shoes, her now pink hair pulled into a high ponytail. Kristen waved as she finished setting carpet squares out in a semi-circle for the children. "Hey, Annabelle, good morning. You ready?"

"Oh, yeah. I'm looking forward to it! Thanks for letting me do story time today." Annabelle came over, holding a copy of *Olivia the Pig* in her hands. "I'm going to start with this one. It's my favorite."

Kristen sat down with Annabelle. She did not doubt that with her flair for the dramatic, along with her kind heart and endless patience, Annabelle's story time would be a hit with the kids. "You're going to do great today."

Just then, Josh came through the front door. Mondays were usually his day off, but he'd offered to cover the coffee bar during story time. He smiled at Kristen and Annabelle as he passed by on his way downstairs to the kitchen. "Good morning, ladies."

Kristen got up from the floor and followed Josh to help him bring up the supplies for the day. As he pulled cartons of milk from the large refrigerator, she asked, "Do you think I should add more almond milk to our grocery order? Are we keeping up okay?"

Josh turned toward Kristen. "I think we're good. You keep this place running like a well-oiled machine. I don't know how you do it all."

"Thank you. I was feeling pretty overwhelmed right after Mary left, but hiring you fixed that. And now, between you, Annabelle, and me, I think we're finding our groove. We're a good team!" His eyes sparkled with amusement, locking onto hers.

Kristen felt her pulse quicken as she thought about their dinner conversation the night before. Last night's late dinner together had brought them closer. She'd told Josh about her family and other parts of herself that she rarely opened up to people about. He'd told her more about his writing and his recent breakup with a woman named Stephanie, who'd been less than supportive of his goals.

Kristen had resolved this morning that the only way this thing with Josh—whatever it was—might work was to keep it separate from their work together at the store. Josh, however, was a flirt, and Kristen, who enjoyed every bit of his attention, already knew this would be easier said than done.

Lugging two gallons of milk upstairs, Kristen shifted her focus back to business.

***

Kristen stood behind the cash register, a satisfied smile playing on her lips. The preschool story hour had been a resounding success. The children, their faces beaming with joy, had gathered around Annabelle as she animatedly read aloud from several picture books. Laughter filled the air, accompanied by the delicious scent of her freshly baked cookies which the kids eagerly munched on. As the parents filed toward the register, arms loaded with books, Kristen greeted them warmly and began ringing up their purchases.

One young mother's eyes landed on *Mrs. Canfield's Cookery Book* sitting near the register. Its aged cloth cover and worn pages exuded a sense of history. "Is that book for sale?" she inquired, pointing.

Kristen's heart skipped a beat, her attachment to the book tightening like a protective grip. She had forgotten to return it to the office. She glanced at the mother; her expression tinged with regret. "I'm sorry; it's not for sale. It belongs to my boss."

The mother's face fell, disappointment etching lines on her forehead. "Oh, I see," she said, her voice tinged with longing. "May I take a little peek?"

Kristen nodded and carefully handed it over, empathizing with the woman's curiosity. Just then, the young mother's little boy, his hands still coated in a thick layer of pink frosting, reached out and snatched the precious book from his mother's hands.

Time seemed to slow as Kristen's heart raced. "No!" Kristen exclaimed, desperation lacing her voice.

The boy's tiny hands opened the book haphazardly, and a smear of sugary delight smudged across the cover and on a delicate page. The mother gasped as her eyes widened in shock.

"Oh, I'm so sorry!" she stammered, her voice laced with apologies. "I didn't mean for this to happen. Please forgive us!"

Kristen tried to hide the horror from her face as she reached out to take the book gently from the boy's hands. "It's alright. Accidents happen," she said as she studied the pink frosting stain on the page, her heart sinking.

The mother's gratitude overflowed, her eyes full of relief. "Thank you for understanding," she murmured, her voice full of appreciation.

Kristen nodded, her gaze returning to the book's stained page. Although the page bore a permanent mark, she knew the value of the book lay not in its physical condition but in the memories and stories it held. Besides, she couldn't blame the kid. The cookbook shouldn't have been left out. She glanced up at the mother and managed to form a weak smile.

After checking out the rest of the customers, Kristen glanced at the clock on the wall. It was noon already. She found Annabelle in the children's area. "You were fantastic!

Thank you so much. Would you like to lead story hour every week for the rest of the summer?"

Annabelle grinned. "Sure. I'd love to!"

"It's all yours, then." Kristen reached for the broom Annabelle was holding. "Here, I'll finish cleaning up. You can go take your lunch break."

Josh left a few minutes later, rushing to make it to his class. For the first time all morning, Kristen was alone in the shop. She straightened a stack of books on the shelf as the tinkling of the bell announced the arrival of a customer. Glancing up, she couldn't help but notice how beautiful the young woman was. With flowing chestnut hair, radiant blue eyes, and flawless skin, the woman resembled a model straight out of a glossy magazine.

Kristen smiled, "Good afternoon. May I help you?"

The woman returned the smile and leaned against the counter, exuding an air of confidence. "Hi there. I'm looking for Josh. Is he still here?"

"I'm sorry, but Josh has already left for the day. Can I help you with anything?"

The woman's eyes sparkled with curiosity. "Oh, that's a shame. I'm Stephanie, by the way. I heard he started working here recently."

A wave of realization washed over Kristen, and she discreetly clasped her hands together to hide her trembling fingers. Standing before her was the woman who had once held Josh's heart.

"It's nice to meet you, Stephanie," Kristen attempted to keep her voice composed and friendly. "I'm Kristen. I'll make sure Josh knows you came by."

Stephanie's smile faltered slightly, her eyes searching Kristen's face. She seemed to sense the tension in the air. "Thank you. It was lovely meeting you, Kristen."

As the bookshop door shut behind Stephanie, a whirlwind of thoughts raced through Kristen's mind. Why was Stephanie looking for Josh? Was it merely a friendly visit, or did it indicate something more? Insecurities gnawed at her.

Kristen sighed. The day had begun so well. She glanced at her watch; two more hours to go before she could close up and go home. For the first time in a while, doubts began to creep in. Was she making good choices for her future? Or was she sabotaging herself?

Kristen

CHAPTER TWELVE

Kristen wearily pushed her shopping cart as she slowly shuffled through the crowded aisles of Winco, her mind still preoccupied with the encounter at the bookshop earlier in the day. All she wanted was to retreat into the solace of her cozy apartment and lose herself in the pages of a good book.

As she rounded the corner into the produce section, her heart skipped a beat at the sight of Josh, who was engrossed in selecting a perfect tomato. He seemed oblivious to her presence as his attention solely focused on the task at hand.

She backed up and peered around the corner, considering her options. Part of her yearned to pretend she hadn't noticed him, to let the tiredness guide her away and escape the complexities that now clouded her thoughts. But deep down, she knew avoiding him wouldn't make her uncertainties disappear.

Just then, Josh's gaze lifted from the tomatoes, and his eyes locked onto hers. Confusion furrowed his brow as he walked toward her.

Kristen's heart raced, and she felt a mix of guilt and apprehension as he approached. How could she explain hiding around the corner without unraveling the inner turmoil left by Stephanie's unexpected visit earlier that day?

Josh's voice carried a tinge of uncertainty as he greeted her. "Hey, Kristen. Are you ... avoiding me?"

Kristen's mind scrambled to find an answer that wouldn't betray her insecurity. She took a deep breath and mustered a weak smile. "Oh, no, not at all. I just ... I was lost in my own thoughts, I guess."

A flicker of confusion lingered in Josh's eyes, but he nodded, a subtle sign that he was willing to accept her explanation—at least for the moment. "Okay. Well, I'm glad I caught you. How was the rest of your day?"

Kristen hesitated, unsure of how much to reveal. She didn't want to burden Josh with her insecurities, but she also didn't want to shut him out completely. "It was ... fine, I guess. Just busy. How about you?"

As they exchanged polite small talk, Kristen couldn't shake the tension that lingered between them.

Their conversation remained superficial, punctuated by uneasy silences until she straightened her shoulders and blurted, "Hey, if you're not already busy tonight, why don't you come over, and I'll fix you dinner?."

Josh put the bag of tomatoes in his cart. "I was just going home to make some salsa, then veg in front of the TV for a while, but that sounds like a lot more fun. Sure! What can I bring?"

***

As Kristen carefully flipped the sizzling pork chops, their tantalizing aroma filling her tiny kitchen, she mentally replayed her conversation with Josh at the grocery store. Had she overreacted? Maybe a conversation with Josh would clear things up. She'd tell Josh that Stephanie had come by the shop and then ask him some clarifying questions.

A knock at the door announced Josh's arrival. Kristen ran to the door, invited Josh into the kitchen, then returned to her spot at the stove. As she placed the tantalizing chops onto a plate, Kristen turned to face Josh, who stood near the kitchen counter. She took a deep breath, summoning the courage to speak. "Josh, I have something to tell you. Earlier today, Stephanie came by the bookstore looking for you."

Josh's gaze met Kristen's, his expression calm and unruffled. "Stephanie? Ah, that's not too surprising. She's moving back home to Portland soon."

Kristen's eyes widened slightly at the revelation. "Moving back to Portland, huh?"

Josh stepped closer, a warm smile spreading across his face. He reached out, gently placing a hand on Kristen's arm. "Stephanie and I? We're ancient history. Kristen, you're the one I've got my eyes on."

A flicker of relief washed over Kristen as the reassurance in his words resonated deeply within her. She had let her insecurities cloud her judgment. She returned his smile. "Well, that's good to know, because I feel the same way about you." She paused a moment before asking, "So, what do you think Stephanie wanted?"

Josh's smile faded slightly, and he let out a sigh. "Look, Kristen, Stephanie and I ... we wanted different things in life. She wanted someone with a more traditional nine-to-five career. You know, something that offers stability and prestige."

Kristen furrowed her brows, puzzled. "I don't get it. What's wrong with being a writer?"

Josh chuckled, running a hand through his hair. "Nothing's wrong with being a writer, and I love what I do. But Stephanie had this idea of a perfect life that didn't quite align with mine. I couldn't give her what she wanted, and I didn't want to compromise who I am for the sake of someone else's expectations."

Kristen nodded slowly, beginning to understand. "So, she wanted someone with more earning potential?"

"Yeah, exactly," Josh replied, a tinge of regret in his voice. "She thought I should aim for something more financially rewarding. But I couldn't let go of my passion for writing. It's who I am, and I didn't want to sacrifice that."

Kristen pondered Josh's words, realizing how they resonated with her own life. Her continued pressure to live up to her family name through academic and career prestige was intense, but she couldn't ignore the growing disconnect between those expectations and her own dreams.

The idea of taking an editing job in New York or going to law school didn't ignite the same fire that running a bookstore did. She had always been drawn to books and reveled in the power of words to create new worlds and perspectives. She wanted to live in a small town like Moscow, and she didn't want to work alone at an office desk all day. Working in a bookstore brought together her love for reading with her desire to nurture close community bonds.

As she looked at Josh, she admired his courage. He hadn't bowed to societal norms or succumbed to someone else's vision of success. He had chosen his path, embracing the uncertainty that came with a writing career. Kristen couldn't help but wonder if she had the same courage within her.

"So," Kristen began, breaking their thoughtful silence, "do you ever regret not conforming to what Stephanie wanted? I mean, do you think you'll ever want that stability?"

Josh looked at her, a soft smile playing on his lips. "I've never regretted staying true to myself. I'd rather struggle to pursue my passion than live a comfortable life that isn't fulfilling."

Kristen absorbed Josh's words and decided it was time to tell Josh more about where she came from. "Expectations ... I can relate. My mother's maiden name is Leland—as in Leland Hotels."

Josh's expression registered surprise, "Oh, yeah? Cool." He grinned. "So, I'm guessing you've traveled to some pretty great places and never had to pay for a hotel room?"

Kristen laughed, "Yep, there were some perks."

"And the downsides?" Josh prompted gently. He was intrigued by the glimpse into Kristen's past, a stark contrast to his own upbringing.

Kristen's smile faded slightly. "There are downsides, certainly. A lot of pressure to live up to the family name, expectations to follow a certain path. I always feel like I'm walking on eggshells, trying to please everyone. It's exhausting."

She paused, taking a sip of her wine "I suppose that's why I admire your independence so much, Josh. You've never let anyone dictate your life. It's inspiring."

"It's not always easy," Josh admitted, "but it's the only way I know how to live. Authenticity is important to me, and I wouldn't trade it for anything."

A comfortable silence settled between them. Finally, Josh decided to ask the question that had been on his mind. "Speaking of living your own truth, has there ever been anyone special in your life? Someone who truly understood your desire to be different?"

Kristen pondered the question. Dating was a topic she hadn't discussed in a long time, but she felt oddly comfortable sharing about it with Josh. "Honestly, no," she confessed. "Relationships have never been my priority. I've been so focused on establishing myself, on proving myself worthy outside of my family name, that I never really felt like I had the time or energy for love."

Josh took a sip of wine. "You're amazing, Kristen. Your family will see that too. I imagine they already do."

They enjoyed the rest of their dinner together, savoring each bite while exchanging lighthearted banter. The tension that had loomed over them earlier began to dissipate, replaced by a sense of renewed closeness. After finishing their meal, they decided to continue their evening with a trip to Howard Hughes, an old-school video rental store down the street. They seemed to have every movie under the sun, along with employees who had extensive knowledge about them all. They strolled through downtown Moscow hand in hand, enjoying the cool evening air. Their laughter carried on the wind as they reminisced about their favorite movies and debated which one to watch that night. Inside the video store, they perused the aisles together, playfully teasing each other over movie choices until they settled on *My Big Fat Greek Wedding*.

Returning to Kristen's apartment, they snuggled together on the couch, with Lavender in between. As the opening scenes unfolded, Kristen leaned against Josh's chest, feeling a sense of contentment wash over her. At that moment, Kristen knew that despite the uncertainties that occasionally plagued her, she and Josh had started writing their own story. And she was excited to see where it led.

A couple of hours later, when the credits rolled on the screen, Kristen reluctantly got up from the couch and gathered their empty ice cream bowls to take to the kitchen. The room was dimly lit, and a comfortable silence enveloped Kristen's apartment.

Josh turned to Kristen, a soft smile playing on his lips. "I should probably get going. We both have a busy day tomorrow."

Kristen nodded, though a tinge of reluctance tugged at her heart. She didn't want this fun evening to end. Before she could voice a response, Josh leaned closer, his eyes searching hers for consent as the air around them became charged with an unspoken desire. Kristen's heart quickened in anticipation.

As if guided by an invisible force, their lips met in a tender, uncertain kiss. Kristen felt a surge of joy that electrified her entire body, causing her to melt into his embrace and return the kiss with equal fervor.

The world around Kristen faded away, leaving only the sensation of Josh's touch, the warmth of his lips against hers. It was a simple yet profound connection, filled with the unspoken promise of what could be.

As they pulled apart, their eyes met once again, and a shared understanding passed between them. Josh's grin mirrored Kristen's. "I really should get going now, but I'll see you tomorrow at the bookstore."

Josh interlaced his fingers with hers as they walked to the door, and then with one last gaze, he bid Kristen goodnight. The door closed softly behind him, leaving Kristen in the quiet embrace of her apartment. She leaned against the door and smiled, her lips still tingling from their shared kiss.

CHAPTER THIRTEEN

The second book club gathering was in full swing. Kristen, Irene, Julie, Heidi, and Matilda sat comfortably around the coffee table in the apartment above the store, their animated discussion punctuated by sips of iced tea. Ruby had called to say she'd be late but was on her way.

The room buzzed with excitement as they delved into the intricacies of Jan Karon's 'In This Mountain,' a book that seemed to have captivated them all. They shared their favorite characters, relished the heartwarming moments, and passionately debated the deeper themes interwoven within the story.

Kristen excused herself and went into the kitchen to fetch the tray of cupcakes she'd made for her new friends. Her heart sank at the sight of Lavender perched on the edge of the table, crumbs scattered everywhere like confetti, and the once-pristine tray of cupcakes now a chaotic mess on the floor.

"Oh no, Lavender!" She shouted, just as Ruby walked into the kitchen.

"Sorry, I'm late ... oh, yikes." Ruby's eyes widened as she took in the scene, then she chuckled. She was holding a plate of chocolate chip cookies. "Well, we won't starve. I brought these."

With a laugh, Kristen gratefully accepted the plate from Ruby, "Ruby, thank you! Would you mind passing out these out to the ladies while I clean up this mess?

After Kristen returned to the group, they continued to dissect the book, sharing their favorite passages and marveling at the author's ability to evoke emotions and create memorable characters.

As the discussion grew more animated, a dense heat settled into the room. Kristen furrowed her brow, feeling beads of sweat forming on her forehead. She glanced towards the air conditioning unit in the window, which sat unusually silent and got up to fiddle with its switches. Unable to get it to crank out cool air, Kristen turned to her guests.

"I'm so sorry, ladies," she said, fanning herself. "It seems the air conditioner isn't working."

Julie chimed in with a smile. "Hey, we can always continue the conversation at my house this evening. I have a pool, and the water temperature will be perfect then. We can cool off and pick up where we left off. Anyone interested?"

The ladies exchanged eager glances and nodded in agreement. Gathering their belongings, they left the apartment, promising to finish the discussion later.

That evening, Kristen got out of her car in front of Julie's house and followed the sound of laughter to the backyard gate. Julie spotted her first, gracefully rising from a lounge chair to offer a warm hug. "Welcome! What can I get you to drink? Iced tea? A soda?"

"Iced tea sounds wonderful. Thank you!"

The cool water was refreshing on that hot summer night, and it felt good to relax in the company of these women. It didn't matter that they were a diverse group in age and experience. The love of books had brought them together, and they were already beginning to form a bond. For the next few hours, Kristen forgot about everything else that was going on in her life while she soaked in the sweet camaraderie of this new sisterhood. Looking around at the women at this impromptu pool party, she was glad the air conditioner had gone out in Mary's apartment that day.

***

Kristen's excitement bubbled over as she chatted with her sister Amy on the phone. The early morning sunlight streamed through the window, casting a warm glow throughout her living room.

"The book club is thriving, Amy." Kristen gushed, "We had a fantastic discussion about the last book, and the ladies absolutely adored it."

"That's amazing, Kristen! I'm so glad you've found something you enjoy so much. What about the bookstore ... and your new employee? What was his name ... Josh? How's everything going there?"

Kristen hesitated a moment, pondering whether to divulge the recent developments in her personal life. But she quickly decided she didn't want to keep anything from her sister.

Taking a deep breath, Kristen let it spill. "It's good. Josh and I have been spending time together, and ... well, we kissed."

"Oh, wow ... how do you feel about that?"

Kristen couldn't help but smile, a warm glow spreading across her face. "It feels right, Amy. Being with Josh is unlike anything I've experienced before. He makes me happy, and I can't help but hope for something more."

As the joy of her budding romance filled her heart, Amy's next question brought Kristen crashing back to reality. "What about Mary? Once she's back from Ireland, what do you plan to do? Are you still considering a move to New York?"

A pang of sadness hit Kristen as she considered her sister's words. She leaned back against the couch, the weight of uncertainty settling upon her. "I don't know, Amy. It's something I've been thinking about. I know Mary will be coming back at some point, and then I'll need to move on, but the thought of leaving Josh and the bookstore behind ... it breaks my heart."

"Change can be difficult, sis. But maybe this was only meant to be a short summer romance ... a break from real life. Have fun, for now."

Kristen sighed. "This is real life, Amy."

"Of course. I didn't mean it like that. But you know what I mean. Right?"

Kristen wasn't sure she did. The conversation was bringing her down. "Yeah ... I've got to go. I need to go to the shop and bake some scones before we open. I'll talk to you later."

"Hey, sis. I'm sorry. I really am. Don't listen to me, and please don't be mad at me. I just don't want your heart to get broken."

Amy sounded sincere. Kristen felt the tense muscles in her shoulders relax. "I know you're just looking out for me. I'm not mad."

"I'm happy for you, Kristen, and I want to hear more about Josh next time we talk. He sounds like a good guy."

"He is."

"Alright. I'll let you go, and I hope you have a good day. Love you!"

"I love you too."

After hanging up the phone, Kristen put Lavender in the cat carrier and left for work. A to-do list ran through her mind as she walked: call a repairman to fix Mary's air conditioner, put in another grocery order for the coffee counter, and run a deposit to the bank. Then she prayed silently, asking God if there was any way she might stay in Moscow for good. And if so, how?

CHAPTER FOURTEEN

A Destiny's Child song loudly played inside Maurice's clothing store as Kristen happily hummed along to "I'm a Survivor." Two days. Two blissful days of stolen glances, whispered jokes, and lingering touches with Josh. A giddy smile tugged at her lips as she browsed the summer dress rack, picturing herself in a breezy sundress on a picnic with him.

Suddenly, a voice laced with a hint of surprise sliced through her daydream. "Kristen? What a coincidence!"

Kristen spun around, her smile faltering as her eyes landed on Stephanie. Standing there, impeccably dressed in a tailored white pantsuit, was Josh's ex-girlfriend. Gone was the casual air she'd displayed at the bookstore; replaced by a controlled elegance that radiated an unspoken challenge.

"Stephanie," Kristen managed, her voice clipped. "Fancy seeing you here."

Stephanie's smile widened, a touch too bright. "Likewise. Picking out a new summer wardrobe?" Her gaze flickered to the dresses Kristen held, then back to her face.

"Just browsing," Kristen mumbled, suddenly self-conscious. The carefree, floral print suddenly seemed too young, too... unrefined compared to Stephanie's polished image.

An awkward silence stretched between them. Kristen shifted her weight, the shopping bags digging into her fingers. She desperately wished she could melt into the clothes rack and disappear.

"So," Stephanie finally drawled, "I hear you and Josh are... an item now?"

Kristen bristled. She hated the way Stephanie phrased it as if they were some fleeting trend. "Yes," she said curtly. We are."

Stephanie's smile faltered for a brief second, a flicker of something Kristen couldn't decipher crossing her eyes. Then, she recovered smoothly. "Well, good for you both. He's a good guy, Josh. Just... a little unconventional sometimes."

There it was again, that veiled condescension. Kristen clenched her jaw. "Unconventional? Like chasing his dreams instead of chasing a corporate paycheck?" She regretted the words the moment they left her lips, but the barb felt necessary.

Stephanie's smile turned strained. "Something like that," she said coolly. "I just hope he doesn't get... sidetracked." Her gaze held a pointed glint.

Kristen's temper flared. "What's that supposed to mean?"

"Nothing," Stephanie said quickly, raising her hands in a placating gesture. "Just... well, I wish you both the best. Truly."

Before Kristen could formulate a retort, Stephanie turned on her heel and walked away, leaving Kristen feeling hollowed out and oddly threatened. The playful dresses in her hand suddenly seemed to mock her. Was Stephanie right? Was Kristen just a temporary detour for Josh, a distraction from the "real" life he should be leading?

Doubt gnawed at Kristen's heart, poisoning the joy of her newfound relationship. She shoved the dresses back on the rack, the carefree evening at the mall now a distant memory. All she wanted to do was find Josh, to hear him say the words that would chase away the shadows Stephanie's visit had cast.

Frustration simmered in Kristen's stomach as she left the mall. Stephanie's pointed words echoed in her mind, leaving a sour taste on her tongue. Reaching for her phone, she dialed Josh's number, needing to hear his voice to dispel the sudden unease gripping her.

"Hey, Kristen," Josh's warm voice filled her ear. Relief washed over her, momentarily pushing back the insecurities Stephanie had stirred.

"Josh," she started, then hesitated. How much should she tell him?

"Everything alright?" His voice held a hint of concern.

Taking a deep breath, Kristen explained her encounter with Stephanie. She recounted their conversation, leaving out the sharper barbs but conveying the underlying tension Stephanie had exuded.

Silence greeted her on the other end of the line. Tension coiled in her gut.

"Josh?" Her voice trembled slightly.

"Yeah, I'm here," he finally said. "Listen, Stephanie actually came by my house earlier today to pick up some things she'd left behind."

Kristen's brow furrowed. "Oh."

"I told her about us," Josh continued. "She... wasn't thrilled, to say the least."

Kristen winced. "I figured."

"But Kristen, listen to me," Josh's voice softened. "The only person I'm interested in right now is you. Stephanie's past. Her expectations of what my life should be... they don't matter anymore. I want to be with you, okay? And after next week, you don't need to worry about running into her anymore. She'll be gone...to Portland."

His sincere and unwavering words washed away the doubts that had crept in, and a genuine smile bloomed on her face.

"Okay," she replied, the single word holding the weight of newfound confidence.

"Good," he chuckled. "So, how about I swing by your place later? I'll bring ice cream and we can watch that Spider-Man movie you've been wanting to see."

The playful suggestion chased away the last vestiges of unease. "Sounds perfect," she said, her voice lighter.

Hanging up, Kristen gazed out the window. Stephanie's visit had been a wake-up call, a reminder of the insecurities Kristen needed to confront. But Josh's reassurance had been a balm, a testament to the connection they were building. Stephanie might not be happy, but Kristen knew, with a newfound certainty, that Josh was worth fighting for. And she, for one, was ready to face whatever came their way.

CHAPTER FIFTEEN

Kristen sat in the small office at the bookshop, eating the sack lunch of cheese, crackers, and fruit she'd brought from home. The familiar scent of coffee wafted in through the open door, providing a sense of comfort amidst the uncertainty that swirled in her mind. As she absent-mindedly flipped through the pages of *Mrs. Canfield's Cookery Book for the Modern Woman*, she paused on a recipe for meatloaf. So far, she'd mostly stuck with the recipes for baked goods, but it might be fun to branch out. Did Josh like meatloaf?

Ground beef, bread crumbs, onion, milk ... Kristen grabbed a scrap of paper and a pen and began a shopping list. A knock on the door startled her. Josh stood there with his backpack slung over his shoulder. "I have to get to class. Annabelle has everything covered upstairs. I just wanted to say goodbye before I left."

"Sure, thanks. Hey, Josh, how about joining me for dinner tonight? I'm experimenting with meatloaf."

"Oh, yeah? That sounds good. Can I bring anything?"

"Just yourself."

Josh glanced behind him, then leaned over the desk and gave her a slow, lingering kiss. When he stood back up, his eyes moved toward the open book on the desk. "I've been meaning to ask, what's the story behind this book? It seems to be important to you."

Kristen smiled. "It is. It's really old, and it's full of stories. I'll show it to you when you come to dinner tonight."

***

That evening, Kristen and Josh found themselves seated at Kristen's small dining table. The tantalizing aroma of meatloaf, rich with herbs and spices, filled the cozy apartment, creating a comforting ambiance. Kristen, wearing an apron splattered with stains from her culinary adventures, glanced at the timer and then at the vintage cookbook resting on the table.

"I hope this meatloaf turns out okay," Kristen said, a touch of uncertainty in her voice. "I've never made it before, and the recipe in this book is a bit of a mystery."

Josh chuckled, a twinkle in his eyes as he reached for Kristen's hand. "Well, even if it doesn't turn out perfectly, I'm sure it'll still be an edible adventure. Besides, I'm here to taste-test and offer moral support."

Kristen smiled gratefully, appreciating his lightheartedness. She flipped open the old cookbook, "Look at this," Kristen said, pointing at a page where someone had underlined a sentence and scribbled a quote in the margin. "It's like a treasure hunt, piecing together the stories behind these annotations."

Josh leaned in; his curiosity piqued. "What does it say?"

Kristen read the passage aloud. "It says, 'Cook with love, and your food will always taste better.' Wise words, indeed."

Together they turned the pages and studied the marginalia—poems, doodles, and even the occasional grocery list. Each mark held a secret history, a glimpse into the lives of those who had once cherished this cookbook.

Finally, they came to the page with the meatloaf recipe. The page was smudged, forcing Kristen to make educated guesses about some of the measurements and ingredients. She shrugged and laughed, realizing the uncertain nature of her endeavor.

"It's like deciphering an ancient manuscript," Josh grinned. "But hey, that's part of the fun, right?"

The timer beeped, and they shared a laugh, their spirits buoyed by the joy of exploration. Kristen carefully removed the meatloaf from the oven, The meat looked somewhat unconventional with its' plum coloring, but they held hope that it would taste delicious.

However, their optimism met with disappointment as the first bite revealed a bland and dry result. Kristen and Josh exchanged glances.

"Well," Kristen said, a mischievous grin spreading across her face, "I guess Mrs. Canfield's meatloaf recipe remains a mystery for now."

Josh chuckled, his eyes twinkling. "Indeed. But hey, we can't let a minor setback ruin our dinner. How about we order some pizza from Pipeline instead?"

Kristen nodded enthusiastically, relief washing over her. They set aside the failed meatloaf, opting for the familiarity of a piping-hot pizza delivery. Their disappointment was quickly forgotten amidst their shared laughter and the anticipation of a tasty meal.

Thirty minutes later, as they sat together enjoying the delicious pizza, Kristen realized that the true joy of the evening lay not in the perfection of the meal but in the shared experience. It was the laughter, the exploration of the mysterious cookbook, and her genuine connection with Josh that was making this an evening to remember.

Kristen leaned back in her chair, feeling relaxed and comfortable. She gazed at Josh thoughtfully and asked, "What was it like growing up here in Moscow?"

A soft, nostalgic smile spread across his face as he took a moment to travel back to his childhood. "I loved it," he replied warmly. "Small-town life has its charm, you know? It's close-knit; everyone knows each other. There's a real sense of community."

Kristen nodded, intrigued by his response. "What were your family and friends like?"

"Well," Josh began, "my mom is still a second-grade teacher at the elementary school here. She's been teaching for as long as I can remember, and she's just as passionate about it now as she was when I was a kid. My dad owns a whitewater rafting company. We used to go on rafting trips all the time when I was younger. It was one of our favorite family activities. Lately, between school and work, I haven't had as much time to go rafting."

Kristen listened attentively, imagining the joy and excitement of those rafting adventures. "And do you have any siblings?"

Josh nodded. "I have one sister. She's five years older than me, married, and has two kids. They moved to Boise a few years ago, but we still stay in touch and visit each other whenever we can."

"It sounds like you have a wonderful family," Kristen said, a warm feeling washing over her. And it sounds like we both love living in Moscow."

Josh's face lit up. "I really do. Growing up here was fun, and I've made so many good memories with my family and friends. I don't think I ever want to leave Moscow. Besides, my dad wants me to take over the company in a few years when he retires, and I'll be able to take advantage of the off season to work on my novels."

The words resonated with Kristen and she felt a sense of peace settling within her. It was refreshing to hear someone so content.

"Staying in Moscow does sound appealing. After spending so many years in school here, it has really started to feel like home for me," Kristen mused, her mind wandering to the future. "I'm not sure what I'll do after Mary comes back and no longer needs me to run the store."

Josh smiled warmly, "Who knows what the future holds? Maybe you'll make Moscow your forever home, too."

Kristen felt a sense of optimism and gratitude as she looked around her apartment and thought about the connections she had made in this town. She didn't know what the future held, but for now, she decided to rest in the present moment and embrace the happiness she felt in this very place.

"I'm happy," Kristen said softly, her eyes meeting Josh's. "And though I don't have all the answers about what's next for me, I'm going to enjoy where I'm at right now."

Josh reached across the table and squeezed her hand gently. "That's the spirit. Enjoy the journey, and everything will fall into place."

CHAPTER SIXTEEN

After church on Sunday, Kristen, Josh, Leah, and Todd decided to head to Wingers for lunch. Nestling into a booth, they perused the menu as cutlery clinked and lively chatter filled the air around them.

After placing their orders, Josh and Todd discussed their shared interest in white water rafting. Kristen listened intently, her own sense of adventure ignited as she imagined the rush of adrenaline and the thrill of conquering the untamed river. But when Todd proposed the idea of going rafting as a group the following weekend, and everyone else was enthusiastic about the plan, Kristen's excitement was dampened by a sense of responsibility.

"That sounds incredible! But Saturdays at the bookstore are usually a madhouse, and if both Josh and I are gone, it only leaves Annabelle to run things. Since she's only sixteen, I think being on her own all day would be a bit too much."

Josh nodded understandingly, his eyes filled with empathy as he reached over to give Kristen's hand a reassuring squeeze. "Oh, right. I didn't think about that. It's frustrating, but we'll figure something out."

Kristen sighed, the weight of the situation settling on her shoulders. This was an unanticipated drawback of dating someone who worked for her: they couldn't take the same days off. Hiring another employee seemed like a logical solution, but she hesitated, unsure of the financial ramifications and how to approach Mary about it. Besides, an extra person would no longer be needed once Mary returned.

As they continued to wait for their food to arrive, frustration brewed within Kristen, intensifying with each passing minute. Once again, she would barely have time to eat before rushing to open the store. She wanted to slow down and relax over the meal, and she wanted to hang out with friends outside of work more often. The excitement she had felt earlier was replaced by a sense of unease and uncertainty. When the food finally arrived, she asked for a to-go box.

"I'm sorry, everyone," Kristen said, her voice tinged with disappointment. "I have to get going. I'm already running late. The store is supposed to open in five minutes."

Josh and Todd exchanged sympathetic glances. "I'll see you later this afternoon," Josh smiled at her. "Don't worry, Kristen. We'll find a solution that works for everyone."

With a hasty goodbye, Kristen left the restaurant, her mind preoccupied with the staffing dilemma and her responsibilities at the bookstore. As she walked through the streets, disappointment gnawed at her, clouding her thoughts. She couldn't help but feel a sense of longing for more flexibility and freedom, but the reality of the situation weighed heavily on her.

The bookstore was wonderful, but she yearned to find a better balance between work and her personal life. Of course, this dilemma was her own making. Her sister had warned her that dating an employee could be problematic. But then again, she wouldn't be Josh's boss for that much longer. Mary would return. And then what? That was still the big question.

Arriving at the bookstore, Kristen unlocked the door and stepped inside. The store was quiet, with only the sound of her footsteps echoing in the empty space as she settled into her work routine.

Later that afternoon, Kristen sat behind the front counter, meticulously organizing book orders for the upcoming fall season. As her fingers flew across the computer keyboard with practiced efficiency, an email notification disrupted her concentration. Furrowing her brows in annoyance, she opened the email and discovered a message from Mary.

Hey Kristen,

I hope this email finds you well. I wanted to share some news and express my gratitude for everything you've done for the store. It looks like my sister's recovery is progressing better than expected, and I believe I'll be able to return to the bookstore by the first week of September. I can't wait to be back!

Your dedication and hard work during my absence have been invaluable, and I want you to know how much I appreciate it. The store has been running smoothly under your management, and I am truly grateful for your efforts.

If there's anything you need or anything we should discuss, please let me know. I value your opinion, and I want to ensure a smooth transition when I come back. You've done an outstanding job, and I want to make sure I support you as best as I can.

Take care, and I look forward to seeing you soon.

Best,

Mary

Kristen reread the email, her emotions warring within her. She was genuinely happy for Mary and her sister's progress, wishing them nothing but the best. However, mixed with her joy was a sense of uncertainty and sadness. Mary's impending return likely meant that Kristen's time as the manager of the bookstore would come to an end. Though she knew this gig was only temporary, she also wished she could stay in her current role despite the sacrifices it sometimes demanded. On the other hand, she could finally hang out with Josh and her friends. But the bookstore held a special place in her heart, and she loved the responsibility and the sense of purpose it provided.

Without hesitation, Kristen clicked the "Reply" button, her fingers dancing across the keyboard.

Hi Mary,

I'm glad to hear that your sister is making progress, and I'm genuinely excited about your return to the bookstore. It will be wonderful to have you back.

Thank you so much for your kind words. It has been an honor to manage the store in your absence, and I'm grateful for the opportunity. Since you asked, I believe it would be helpful to have some additional part-time help, especially during the remaining summer months. Perhaps hiring another student who can work until the end of the season would alleviate some of the workload.

I truly value my time at the bookstore, and I also want to ensure a smooth transition when you return. If there's anything else we need to discuss or plan, please let me know. I'm here to support you and the store in any way I can.

Looking forward to your return.

Best,

Kristen

Kristen pressed the "Send" button, and a mix of hope and uncertainty surged within her. Now, it was a waiting game. Whatever the outcome, she would make the best of it.

Putting the email aside, Kristen vowed to give the bookstore her all, regardless of the circumstances, and turned her attention back to the computer screen. After completing the book orders, she took down the early summer window display and put everything away. Since there weren't any customers to serve, she returned to the front desk and absentmindedly opened the email program. She was surprised to see a new message from Mary in the inbox.

Excitement mingled with trepidation as Kristen opened the email, her heart pounding in her chest.

Kristen,

I appreciate your input and support. I think hiring another part-time employee—a high school student until the end of summer—is a great idea. Feel free to proceed with the hiring process. Let's ensure we have a smooth transition and the support needed when I come back.

Take care, and keep up the fantastic work!

Best,

Mary

Fueled with renewed determination, Kristen closed her email and began gathering items for the new window display as she contemplated the possibilities that awaited her.

CHAPTER SEVENTEEN

The apartment above the bookshop was abuzz with laughter and animated conversation as the book club ladies gathered for their weekly meeting. Thank goodness the air conditioning is fixed, Kristen thought as she finished arranging the snacks in Mary's kitchen and brushed a crumb from her sleeveless shirt. Heidi, Matilda, Irene, Julie, and Ruby were already engrossed in conversation, discussing their recent or upcoming vacations and sharing tales of their adventures.

Kristen joined the circle of women, feeling the warmth and camaraderie that always enveloped their gatherings. When the topic of vacations came up, she couldn't help but let out a wistful sigh. "Oh, how I could use a vacation right about now," she admitted, a touch of longing in her voice. "If any of you know of a high schooler who might be interested in a summer job, please let me know."

Matilda turned to Kristen, a thoughtful expression on her face. "My daughter Sasha is looking for a part-time job. She's a responsible high school student and I'm sure she'd be interested in working at the bookstore."

A glimmer of hope sparked in Kristen's eyes as she considered the possibility. She knew Sasha. She was one of Annabelle's friends and a frequent customer who loved Harry Potter and coffee. "That sounds wonderful, Matilda. I'd be more than happy to talk to Sasha about the job. It could be a great opportunity for her and a much-needed help for me."

The conversation continued, laughter and chatter filling the room, and eventually, they even got around to discussing their latest book. As the meeting drew to a close, Kristen announced that their next selection, *The Time Traveler's Wife*, had been recommended by Mary.

Heidi moved forward on the couch with excitement. "I loved that book, and I'll happily read it again! By the way, when is Mary coming back?"

"Her plan right now is to return by September."

"And we'll continue with book club when she returns, right?" Irene asked.

Kristen hadn't thought that far ahead yet. "I imagine so. Mary has been an enthusiastic supporter of this book club from afar, even offering to let us meet in this space."

Later, after the ladies left and Kristen returned downstairs, Annabelle approached her at the coffee bar with a request. "Kristen, I was hoping to take some time off next month to go on vacation with my family. Is that possible?"

A sinking feeling tugged at Kristen's heart. She realized that even with the potential addition of another employee, the timing still might not align for her to get away from the store for a day of rafting. She took a moment to gather her thoughts, trying to hide her disappointment. "Yes, of course. We can make that work. Just let me know the days you'll be gone."

Relief washed over Annabelle's face, gratitude shining in her eyes. "Thank you, Kristen. I really appreciate it. We're going to Seaside, Oregon, and I've really been looking forward to it."

Kristen smiled. She was happy for Annabelle. Really. Kristen would just have to wait a bit longer for her own time away.

The bell above the door jingled as Sharon, the owner of the toy store across the street, stepped into the bookstore.

Pausing from her work at the espresso machine, Kristen looked up and greeted Sharon with a warm smile. "Good afternoon, Sharon. The usual latte?"

Sharon nodded with a grateful smile. "Yes, please, Kristen. And make it extra foamy today."

As Kristen prepared the latte, Sharon leaned against the counter, her eyes scanning the display of freshly baked scones. "You know, Kristen, these scones of yours are simply delightful. I can't resist grabbing a couple every time I come in. I'll take two more. How are you holding up with Mary being away?"

Kristen sighed softly, handing Sharon the foamy latte. "It's been challenging, I won't lie. I miss her guidance and support, especially when it comes to handling the day-to-day operations. But I have an amazing team helping me out. Annabelle and Josh have been a huge help in keeping things running smoothly."

Sharon took a sip of her latte, savoring the taste. "Well, you're all doing a great job. The store is running smoothly, and your scones are divine."

Kristen was genuinely touched by the compliment. "Thank you, Sharon. That means a lot."

Sharon chuckled, leaning casually against the counter. 'Being a business owner has its perks—you're the boss, so you can make your own rules. I'm closing my toy store next week to go on vacation with the family. It's something I couldn't do when I was working for someone else. Now I can do what I want." Sharon paid for her coffee and scones, then waved goodbye.

Kristen couldn't help but feel a pang of envy. The idea of having the freedom to close the store and take a break was appealing, so she allowed her thoughts to drift to the possibility of owning her own business. Maybe someday.

The bell above the door rang again, drawing her attention. Matilda's daughter, Sasha, stepped just inside the entrance, her eyes shyly scanning the bookstore. Kristen smiled warmly and waved her over. "Hi, Sasha! Your mother told me you were interested in a job. Want to sit down so we can talk about it?"

Sasha nodded, her eyes brightening with anticipation. As they settled at a small table near the counter, Kristen sensed Sasha's nervousness and did her best to put Sasha at ease. After chatting about Sasha's interests and school, Kristen shared what her duties would include at the store. She was impressed by the girl's enthusiasm and eagerness to help, even if she was young and inexperienced.

After their conversation, Kristen was confident Sasha would be a good addition to the team. She looked into Sasha's eyes and smiled. "I'd love to give you a chance, Sasha. How about you start next week? We can figure out your schedule and go from there."

Sasha's face lit up with excitement and gratitude. "Thank you so much, Kristen! I promise I'll work hard and do my best."

"I have no doubt about that. I'm looking forward to having you on the team."
As Sasha left with a smile, Kristen felt a renewed sense of optimism.

***

Kristen poured food into Lavender's dish, set it on the floor, and smiled as the cat nuzzled its soft head against her hand, a gesture that seemed to represent "thank you."

"You're a sweet little thing," Kristen cooed, scratching Lavender behind the ears. The cat purred contentedly with its eyes half-closed.

Dawn Klinge

It was just the two of them, alone in the basement kitchen, engaged in what was now a familiar routine of making scones before anyone else arrived. After doubling and quadrupling the original recipe to keep up with demand, Kristen now began her days earlier than ever. What they really needed was a commercial oven that could handle multiple trays at a time, but that would have to wait. She didn't want to burden her boss by asking for any more big expenditures. Mary had thus far been amenable, but she didn't want to push it.

The first batch of scones was underway, so Kristen pulled out her cell phone and called her sister. Amy answered on the first ring, "Hey, sis, what's up?"

Kristen could hear the hissing sound of a latte being made in the background. "Just getting ready to start my day with a cup of coffee. What's your morning beverage of choice?" Kristen asked, taking a sip from her mug.

"Soy hazelnut latte ... hold on." There was a pause, then a jostling, followed by a muffled exchange between Amy and presumably the barista. "Sorry about that," Amy said. "I'm walking outside now."

"Are you enjoying the new job?"

"It's a whirlwind, but I'm learning so much and having a blast! How's the bookstore treating you? Are you still tempted to join me in the bustling metropolis?" Amy teased.

Kristen chuckled. 'As much as I'd love to join you in New York and experience the city that never sleeps, I think I have a fondness for my quiet little town. The bookstore keeps me on my toes, but I'm starting to feel like I'm making a difference," Kristen admitted.

"Making a difference, huh? Does this have anything to do with that cute guy—your new hire?"

"Josh?" Kristen sighed. She didn't want to hear Amy's disapproval, but she also didn't want to have any secrets with her sister. "I do like Josh, and yes, we've gone out a few times, but it's more than that. It's hard for me to imagine moving away from Moscow. In fact, I turned down a job in New York with Simon and Schuster because this is my home."

Amy's voice crackled with surprise. "Wait, what? You turned down a job in New York? Why would you do that? Is this why you kept extending your university studies—to avoid leaving Moscow?"

Kristen's shoulders slumped. "Maybe," she admitted. "I wish I had the same clarity and certainty you have, Amy. You seem to know exactly what you want and where you're headed."

Amy's voice took on a lecturing tone. "Kristen, you can't let fear dictate your life. New York is a city brimming with possibilities; a place where dreams can take flight. You've always expressed a desire for something bigger, and now when that chance is within your grasp, you're holding back."

Kristen furrowed her brow, her voice laced with frustration. "It's not about fear Amy. It's about me finding my place in the world. And right now, I feel like I have made strides and found my footing in Moscow."

Amy's voice softened, a hint of empathy creeping in. "I understand your hesitation, Kristen. But remember those childhood dreams we shared? Dreams of conquering the world together? This is our chance to make those dreams a reality. Moscow may be your comfort zone, but it's not the whole world."

Kristen's lips curled into a faint smile as she recalled their childhood aspirations. "Times change, Amy. Your dreams led you to the bustling streets of New York, and I'm proud of you. Mine, for now, are telling me to stay rooted in the familiarity of Moscow."

A disappointed sigh escaped Amy's lips. "I just don't want you to look back with regret, Kristen. And what about Josh? Is he part of your decision to stay?"

Kristen hesitated, choosing her words carefully. "Josh is great, and I can't deny he's a part of my life here. But even if things don't work out between us, it's not the sole reason I'm thinking of staying close by. I don't know; it just feels right, Amy."

When Amy remained silent, Kristen continued. "Being a member of the Leland family, I've always felt pressured to do something important with my life, like I had to prove I belonged. I don't blame any of you—I put the pressure on myself—but I'm starting to see things differently. I no longer care what other people think because I've learned that what's important is not always measured by outward success." She paused. "Well, I *do* care, but ... oh, I don't know. I'm still sorting it all out in my head."

When Amy spoke, her tone was more understanding. "Okay, I hear you. Just promise me you'll think about it some more. Maybe visit me in New York for a week or two to see how it feels. You don't have to make any decisions right away."

Kristen nodded, even though Amy couldn't see her. "I promise I'll think about it and maybe plan a visit. But, Amy, I need you to support whatever decision I make, even if it means staying in the Northwest."

"Of course I'll support you. Oh, hey, I gotta go. Talk later!"

After Kristen hung up the phone, she sat for a while longer with her coffee, staring into space, thinking about the conversation that had just transpired. She didn't like letting Amy or anyone in her family down, and she was pretty sure she just had.

By noon, the shop was buzzing with activity. A steady stream of customers flowed in and out, their orders demanding her attention. The whirlwind of tasks was a welcome distraction that kept her mind from replaying her morning telephone exchange with Amy.

When a brief lull finally settled over the coffee bar, Kristen sought out Sasha. She found her in the children's room, meticulously arranging the shelves with colorful books and toys.

"Sasha," Kristen said with a smile, "I just wanted to say again how grateful I am that you agreed to work here. You've been a wonderful addition to our team, and I'm so impressed with your work ethic and dedication. How are you feeling about everything so far?"

Sasha looked up from her task, her face lighting up with a wide grin. "Everything's great, Kristen," she replied enthusiastically. "I really enjoy working here. The atmosphere is friendly and the customers are lovely."

Kristen's heart swelled with satisfaction. Sasha's positive attitude and eagerness to learn were refreshing, and she was genuinely happy to have her on board. "I'm so glad to hear that, Sasha. I need to run downstairs and catch up on some paperwork in the office, but feel free to take your lunch break in half an hour."

As Kristen descended the stairs to her office, She paused at her desk, taking a deep breath before clicking on the message.

> *Hey Kristen,*
> *I've been thinking about our conversation this morning and realize I came across as insensitive. I'm sorry. I can now see what you were trying to*

*say to me, and I should have listened
better. Please forgive me.*

*Of course, I want to have my sister
with me in New York because I love
you and miss you, but what I want
more is for you to be happy. And I will
support you—whatever you decide to
do.*

*I want to meet Josh. It sounds like
he's a good guy. Tell me more about
him!*
Love, Amy

Kristen read the email twice, each time absorbing
Amy's genuine remorse and love. A warm feeling
spread through her chest, easing the lingering tension
from their earlier exchange. Amy's apology was not
just about admitting her mistake; it was also a
reaffirmation of their sisterly bond—a reminder of the
unwavering love and support they shared.

Kristen leaned back in her chair, her eyes
fluttering shut. The image of Amy's smiling face filled
her mind, and a wave of longing washed over her. She
missed her sister terribly. She especially missed their
spontaneous chats, shared laughter, and unwavering
support of each other.

With renewed determination, Kristen resolved to
bridge the distance between them. She would reach out
to Amy, plan a visit, and make more time for those
long, heartfelt conversations that had always been a
cornerstone of their relationship. She would nurture
their sisterhood, ensuring that their bond remained
strong and unbreakable, no matter how many miles
separated them.

The challenge would be finding the time. If she couldn't even get away from the store for one day of rafting, how was she supposed to fit in a trip to New York?

It was quiet in the office. With her eyes still closed, Kristen began to pray. *Please, God, show me if I'm on the right track—and if so, please show me what I need to do next.*

Feeling more at peace than before, she went back upstairs.

Kristen went to find Josh, who needed to leave for his afternoon class. Since Annabelle had the day off, Kristen would be alone for the last hour of the workday. Hopefully, the store would be relatively quiet.

Josh was at the cash register, and he smiled when she approached. "I'm going now, but would you like to go for a bike ride tonight after work?"

Kristen returned his smile. "I'd love to. Meet at the park around seven?"

Josh nodded and clocked out. "Seven it is," he confirmed. See you then."

With a final wave, Josh headed out the door, leaving Kristen to anticipate their upcoming bike ride.

CHAPTER EIGHTEEN

A gentle summer evening unfolded, embracing Kristen and Josh with a refreshing breeze as they leisurely pedaled along the scenic Palouse Trail. The wheat fields rustled softly, and birds chirped in the distance, providing a serene backdrop. When they reached a quiet spot with a bench, they got off their bikes to take a break. Kristen took a sip of water before breaking their comfortable silence.

"You know, Josh," she began, "I've started praying and thinking about opening my own bookstore and bakery after Mary comes back."

Josh turned to her with a smile. "Really? That sounds amazing, Kristen. You'd be awesome doing something like that. If it's something you feel passionate about, I'm right here to support you."

His words sent a warm ripple through her, and she couldn't help but smile. "Thank you, Josh. Your support means the world to me. There's still a lot to figure out, and I'm not even sure yet if it's just a passing idea that will go away. You're the first person I've told." She paused a moment before tentatively continuing. "I wouldn't want to compete with Mary, so I'd probably have to open a store somewhere besides Moscow."

His fingers intertwined with hers, offering a reassuring squeeze that spoke volumes without words. "I get that. Of course, selfishly, I'd love for you to stay in Moscow, but I'm happy to bounce ideas around with you ... and I'll be praying for you."

As they got back on their bikes and continued the ride, Kristen found herself pondering Josh's reaction. Their relationship was still so new. It was too soon to discuss any kind of future together. She knew Josh would eventually take over his dad's rafting business, so it made sense that his life would remain in Moscow. He'd been supportive of her idea, and he'd also said he wanted her to stay in Moscow, but Kristen struggled to decipher Josh's true feelings, unsure if he genuinely wanted her to stay. She would have liked it if he had pushed back a little harder against the suggestion of her leaving. Kristen shook her head as if she could empty it of the questions floating around her mind, then shifted her focus to her legs, propelling them into a faster pace.

The final mile into the nearby town of Pullman was a good-natured race between Kristen and Josh, and Kristen won. Before turning back towards Moscow, Kristen noticed that her tire had gone flat. Neither of them had a repair kit with them. Josh's calm demeanor remained unwavering, 'It's easier to talk when we're walking, anyway."

It was just another example of why she admired him. He was consistently calm and easy-going. The downside, in Kristen's view, was this also made him hard to read. The time flew by quickly as they walked and talked, pushing their bikes along the trail.

After a while, Josh reached into his backpack and pulled out two Clif bars, handing one to Kristen. "Here, do you want peanut butter or chocolate chip?"

"Oh, thank you! Chocolate chip, please."

As she savored the energy bar, Kristen thought about work—making scones and lattes—and the looming need for more supplies. They were getting low on chocolate chips.

"Hey, how did it go working with Sasha at the coffee bar today?" she asked.

"She's a quick learner. I think it went well. I hope I didn't overwhelm her too much with everything I showed her."

"Thank you for training her. She's a sweet girl." Kristen paused, then laughed. "Sorry, I'll stop talking about work!"

Josh smiled. "You're fine, and I don't mind. The bookstore is important to both of us."

By the time they reached Josh's Subaru in the parking lot, the stars had begun to twinkle above them. Josh opened the car door for Kristen, and as he loaded the bikes onto the rack, Kristen relaxed. She was happy and tired, and though she wasn't ready to say it yet, she was completely in love with Josh.

When Josh stopped in front of her apartment, she kissed him before getting out of the car. the words lingered on the tip of her tongue, almost escaping into the night air, but she held back, waiting for Josh to make the first move. But she was an old-fashioned girl and wanted to hear him say it first. She couldn't help but wonder—did he love her, too? The way he kissed her back made her think he did, but all he said was, "Goodbye. That was fun. See you tomorrow."

The soft glow of the lamplight filled Kristen's apartment as she stepped inside. Lavender ran to greet her, purring as she rubbed against her legs. The evening had been wonderful, but now she felt a mixture of contentment, confusion, and excitement.

As she hung her jacket on the hook, she noticed the blinking light on her answering machine. Her curiosity piqued, she pressed the playback button, and her mother's familiar voice filled the room.

"Hi, sweetheart. I hope I'm not calling too late. I just wanted to hear your voice and learn how you're doing. It's been a while since we caught up. Anyway, give me a call when you get this. Love you, bye."

A wave of warmth and longing washed over Kristen as she listened to the message. She missed her mom more than she realized, and the thought of sharing the bookstore idea with her was both comforting and nerve-wracking.

Kristen would need her parents' support if she wanted to open a bookstore. She had the necessary funds in a trust, but that money was inaccessible until her thirtieth birthday—unless her parents signed off on the plan. Would they?

Looking at the clock, she saw that it was already ten thirty. She debated whether to call back right then or wait until the morning. While she knew her mom wouldn't mind, she still needed some time to gather her thoughts and muster up the courage to discuss her new idea.

Kristen strolled to the window and fixed her gaze on the star-studded night. She took a deep breath before letting a sigh escape her lips. She expected her mom's support, yet nervousness lingered as she contemplated sharing such a significant step in her life.

"Tomorrow morning," she whispered to herself. "I'll call her first thing. I can do this."

Reassured by her decision, Kristen headed to her bedroom and settled into bed. As she lay there, her mind swirled with thoughts of the future—of her dream bookstore and bakery and her romance with Josh. The possibilities and uncertainties were both thrilling and daunting.

CHAPTER NINETEEN

The morning light filtered through the basement kitchen's windows as Kristen moved with purpose, her hands deftly mixing the scone dough. Weeks of repetition had made this early morning baking routine second nature by now, and she could let her thoughts wander as she worked.

After expertly arranging the scones on the baking tray and placing them in the oven, Kristen reached for her phone. Her fingers trembled slightly as she dialed her mother's number.

The line rang a few times before her mother's sleepy voice greeted her. "Hello?"

"Hi, Mom. It's Kristen," she replied, her voice a mix of nerves and determination.

"Kristen, dear. It's so early. Is everything okay?"

Kristen took a deep breath, her fingers tapping on the kitchen counter. "Oh, yeah ... I guess it is kind of early. I'm sorry; I got your message last night, but I thought it was probably too late to call you back then. Everything's fine; work has been keeping me busy. But I do want to talk to you about something."

There was a pause on the other end, and Kristen could almost picture her mother's concerned expression. "Alright, go on."

"I've been thinking," Kristen began, her voice gaining confidence as she spoke, "about opening my own bookstore and bakery."

Her mother's response was measured. "That's quite a big step, Kristen. Opening a business takes a lot of planning and resources."

"I know, Mom. That's why I wanted to talk to you. I've been thinking about using my trust money to fund the venture."

There was a noticeable pause, and Kristen's heart raced as she waited for her mother's reaction. "Your trust fund ... Kristen, that's a significant decision. And that money is to be held until you're thirty."

"I understand, Mom, but you and Dad can release it early, right?" Kristen replied hopefully. " I'm willing to put in the hard work and effort to make it successful. I truly believe it could be something special."

Her mother's voice softened slightly. "Kristen, this is a big conversation. We can't decide something like this over the phone. Why don't you come to Seattle for the weekend? We can talk it over, discuss your plans, and figure out what's best."

A pang of disappointment hit Kristen. Despite her desire for a face-to-face conversation, the timing just wasn't right. "I appreciate the offer, Mom, but I can't make it to Seattle right now. With Mary away, I'm managing the bookstore on my own. I can't leave until she's back."

There was a moment of silence before her mother spoke again. "I understand. Well, we'll have to find a time that works for both of us to sit down and talk about this in more detail. Maybe your dad and I can make a trip to Moscow. I'll talk to him."

"Of course, Mom. It would be fun to have you both come to visit ... and to see the bookstore."

Her mother's tone softened. "I'm proud of you, Kristen. I'm glad you've found something that has made you so happy. Let's talk more soon. Love you."

"Love you too, Mom."

As Kristen ended the call, a mix of emotions swirled within her. Her mother's lukewarm response hadn't surprised her, and she knew she had a challenging road ahead to convince her parents that opening her own bookstore was a good decision. Taking a deep breath, she removed the scones from the oven and took them upstairs.

With the pastry case fully stocked, Kristen leaned against the counter and checked her watch: twenty minutes until opening. Had it been impulsive to bring up the bookstore idea this morning? Kristen questioned herself, realizing she hadn't thought it through thoroughly. But she knew, as clearly as she'd ever known anything, it was what she wanted. Yet without a solid plan in place, how could she expect her parents to take her seriously? She needed their support, and she needed a plan.

The rest of the day flew by with a steady stream of customers. Kristen didn't have time to think about anything but work ... until Josh invited her to his house for dinner. She looked forward to it but was also nervous. Josh lived in a backyard casita at his parents' house, so there was a high likelihood she'd meet them tonight.

***

As the sun began to dip below the horizon, Kristen followed the backyard path until she found herself standing in front of Josh's casita. With her heart beating just a little faster, she took a deep breath and knocked on the door. Almost immediately, Josh swung the door open, his eyes lighting up in a warm welcome as he ushered her inside. "Hey there, you found it!"

"Of course," Kristen smiled, stepping into the tidy living space. The one-room casita exuded charm, its walls adorned with rustic furniture and bookshelves brimming with well-loved volumes. Josh had created a warm and homey atmosphere.

"Come on in," Josh offered, leaning down to kiss her lightly.

"Thanks," Kristen said, exhaling slowly as she took in the inviting ambiance, feeling her nerves dissipate. "Your place is amazing, Josh. I love the rustic charm, especially those vintage bookshelves. It feels so inviting."

Josh chuckled, "Thanks. I try to keep it organized. With the small size, it only takes about five minutes to clean. Do you want to eat outside by the pool?"

The backyard was an oasis, complete with a sparkling pool and lush foliage. Josh had prepared a spread of sandwiches and sides on the poolside table, and the aroma of the freshly baked bread was mouthwatering.

"This looks delicious Josh," Kristen said, genuinely impressed as she took a seat.

"Well, I don't know how to make much other than sandwiches, to be honest, but I'm glad you like it."

They settled in, and conversation flowed easily as they discussed Kristen's idea for her bookstore and bakery. "You've got the skills and passion, Kristen. A business plan sounds like a good next step. I did my undergrad in business, so if you need any help writing it, I'm here for you."

Just then, the sound of a car pulling into the driveway caught their attention. Josh glanced over and smiled. "Looks like my mom's home."

Kristen's nerves flared up again as she turned to see a beautiful, tall, middle-aged woman approaching them with a kind smile on her face. "Hello, you must be Kristen. I'm Claire. Josh has told me so much about you."

"Hi. Yes, I'm Kristen," she replied, feeling a mixture of relief and warmth in Claire's presence.

"It's lovely to finally meet you," Claire said, extending her hand. "I'm sorry, Jeff, Josh's father, had to work late tonight. I know he's looking forward to meeting you as well."

"Thank you," Kristen said, shaking Claire's hand. "Your backyard is absolutely beautiful."

Claire laughed, her eyes twinkling. "Oh, well, we try to keep it nice, and I love to garden. I hope you two are enjoying your dinner."

"We are. Josh made some delicious sandwiches," Kristen said, feeling more at ease with each passing moment.

Claire excused herself and disappeared into the main house. A few moments later, she returned, cradling a bottle of wine. She poured a glass for all of them, her easy conversation creating a relaxed atmosphere. She turned her attention to Kristen. "So, Kristen, tell me about yourself."

"Right now, I manage the bookstore downtown," Kristen replied, feeling a sense of pride as she spoke. "It's been quite the adventure, especially with Mary being away."

"Oh, yes. Josh told me. Running a business isn't for the faint of heart," Claire said with genuine sincerity, and Kristen couldn't help but feel a warm connection forming. "And what brought you to Moscow? Are you a student?"

"I was. I earned my master's degree in May," Kristen explained.

Claire smiled. "Congratulations! I'm glad you were able to stick around a little longer. Most of the students leave as soon as school lets out for the summer."

As the evening gradually wound down, the temperature dropped slightly, Claire stood and excused herself from the table. "I'll leave you two to enjoy your evening. It was wonderful meeting you, Kristen."

"It was lovely to meet you too, Claire," Kristen replied, touched by the warmth of her hospitality.

Claire turned to Kristen, her eyes conveying warmth, and she pulled her into a genuine hug. "Take care, dear. We'll see you again soon."

Kristen felt a sense of comfort and contentment as they exchanged goodbyes. The evening had gone well.

CHAPTER TWENTY

A week had passed since Kristen first brought up the topic of opening a bookstore to her mother, and now her parents were on their way to see her. Excitement and nerves mingled within her as she drove to the small airport in Moscow to pick them up. The thought of discussing her business idea with her parents weighed heavily on her mind as she mentally rehearsed what she would say to them.

Parking her car near the exit, Kristen scanned the arriving passengers until she spotted her parents, both of them looking slightly tired but happy. She greeted them with a tight hug, feeling a rush of comfort at their familiar presence.

"Hey Mom and Dad. It's wonderful to see you."

"It's good to see you too, sweetie," her mom replied, returning the hug with a gentle squeeze.

Once settled into Kristen's car, her dad got straight to the point. "So, Kristen, your mom tells me you've been thinking about opening a bookstore. Is that right?"

Kristen's heart rate quickened, and she could feel a flush creeping up her neck. She glanced at her father in the passenger seat, his expression cautious and curious. "Yes, that's true. It's an idea I've been contemplating."

Her dad's tone was measured. "Kristen, it's a significant undertaking. Have you considered all the details and challenges that come with running your own business?"

"Yes, I know. But truthfully, I've been running a business all summer, even if it's for someone else. I know it's not easy, but I still love it. I've put a lot of thought into it and even drafted a business plan. I'd like to share it with you back at the apartment."

Her mom chimed in, her voice gentle. "Sweetheart, we just want you to be sure about this. It's important to have a clear plan."

Kristen nodded, feeling a knot forming in her stomach. She had thought it through—or at least she believed she had. But now, as her parents questioned her, the second-guessing began. Was she making a mistake and setting herself up for failure? She was relieved when her dad changed the topic, and the rest of the ride home was spent catching up on what was happening with various extended family members.

Once inside her apartment, her mother reached into her handbag and pulled out a small gift-wrapped box with a gold bow. Betsy Borstad's steadfast rule was never to arrive at someone's house without a gift—no exceptions, not even for family.

"Just a little something for you," she handed the box to Kristen, her eyes roaming around the apartment. "You've got this place decorated so cute!"

Kristen untied the bow and withdrew a sandalwood-scented candle from the box. "Thank you! This smells wonderful."

Kristen offered her parents something to drink and a seat at her kitchen table then smiled and slid the business plan toward her father. He gave a nod, reached for his glasses, and began to read while Kristen and her mother made dinner plans.

Since her parents would only be in Moscow for about twenty-four hours, Kristen had left Josh in charge of the bookstore so she could spend the day with them. She would have liked to have introduced them to Josh at dinner that night, but since he had an evening class on Mondays, she planned to introduce them to Josh at the store. She was still trying to decide how much to share about her relationship with him.

Kristen got up and brought a plate of chocolate chip scones to the table. "These are the scones I've been making for the coffee bar at the store. I'd love to take you there this afternoon so you can see it."

Her mother nodded approvingly as she chewed a mouthful of scone. "Oh, wow, honey ... these are delicious!"

Kristen's father reached for a second scone. "These are delicious! Let's definitely visit the store. I'd like to see it. I just want to finish reviewing the business plan first, then we can discuss it over dinner."

A few minutes later, Kristen and her parents left her apartment. It was a pleasant stroll through the small town with the warm afternoon sun cooled by a soft breeze. She hoped that when her parents saw the store, they would understand her vision and maybe, just maybe, support her in her dream.

As they walked, conversation flowed easily. Kristen's parents asked about her life in Moscow, her friends, and her job managing the bookstore.

"Kristen, you invested two years in earning a master's degree," her dad commented "How do you plan to utilize it?"

His unexpected question pierced Kristen's heart like an arrow and hung in the air, loaded with implications. She tightened her grip on the strap of her bag as a rush of emotions flooded her senses. She had asked herself the same question countless times, but hearing it from her dad only amplified her internal doubts.

"I..." Kristen's voice wavered, and she struggled to find the right words. "I've been thinking a lot about that, Dad. I'm not sure yet, but I believe that my experiences have shaped me, even if they don't seem directly related to running a bookstore."

Her dad nodded, but uncertainty lingered in his eyes. "And something else ... your business plan didn't indicate where you will open this new store. Will it be in Seattle? Are you coming home? I really hope so. At least there, you'd be close by if you need extra support."

Home? Moscow felt most like home to Kristen, not Seattle. And she did have support here—not family, but friends who felt a lot like family. "I don't know. I'm still trying to figure that part out."

As they reached the bookstore, Kristen's thoughts shifted to the pending introduction between her parents and Josh. She wanted them to meet him, but she also felt anxious about how it might unfold. She led them into the store, the familiar scent of books and freshly ground coffee welcoming them as they walked to where Josh stood at the sales counter.

"Mom, Dad, meet Josh. He's part of our team," Kristen announced, gesturing toward him."

"Nice to meet you both," Josh said as he greeted them with a warm smile and a handshake.

Nevertheless, Kristen could sense a slight tension in the air, and her heart sank. She had introduced Josh as if he were just another co-worker, and she could tell that Josh's feelings were hurt by the way his smile didn't quite reach his eyes. When a customer approached the counter, Josh turned his attention to ringing up the sale. Kristen knew she had messed up, and a wave of regret washed over her.

After showing her parents around the rest of the store and noting that Josh was still busy, she led them back home. Kristen's mind was a whirlwind of thoughts, her inner turmoil almost drowning out the conversation with her parents.

As they walked, Kristen decided that honesty was the best approach. She took a deep breath, her voice tinged with sincerity. "Mom, Dad, I need to be honest with you about something. Josh ... he's not just a co-worker. We're in a relationship, and I'm sorry I didn't introduce him properly."

Her parents glanced at each other, surprise evident in their expressions. Kristen could feel the weight of their unspoken questions, concern, and perhaps even judgment.

Kristen continued with her gaze fixed on the ground. "I care about him a lot, and I want you to know that."

Her mom spoke gently, "Kristen, we appreciate your honesty. We only want what's best for you. It seems you have a lot of big changes happening in your life right now."

The silence stretched between them until her father cleared his throat.

"Kristen," he began, his voice measured and calm. "We're surprised by this, of course. We haven't known anything about Josh, and ... well, we just want to understand what's going on."

He paused, his gaze searching hers. "Can you tell us more about him? About your relationship?"

Kristen felt a lump forming in her throat, but she knew she owed them an explanation. She took a deep breath and launched into a hesitant explanation of how she and Josh had grown close while working in the bookstore, sharing their dreams and fears, and finding solace in each other's company.

As she spoke, her voice gained strength, fueled by her love for Josh and her conviction in their relationship. She told them about his intelligence, his humor, his unwavering support, and his shared passion for literature.

Her parents listened intently, their expressions softening as they caught a glimpse into the depths of her feelings. When she finished, a long silence followed, filled only with the rustling of leaves and the distant chirping of birds.

Finally, her mother broke the silence, her voice soft and understanding. "Kristen, we love you very much, and we just want you to be happy. If Josh makes you happy, then we'll support your relationship."

A wave of relief washed over Kristen. She had anticipated a much harsher reaction, and the outpouring of love and support from her parents felt like a warm embrace.

"However," her father added, his voice laced with gentle concern, "we would like to get to know Josh better. We want to spend some time with the man who has captured your heart."

Kristen's heart swelled with gratitude. This wasn't the rejection she had feared. Instead, it was an opportunity. An opportunity to bridge the gap between her two worlds by sharing her love with the people who mattered most to her.

"Of course," she replied, a genuine smile gracing her lips. "I would love for you to meet him properly. Perhaps we can all have dinner together sometime soon?"

As they continued walking, Kristen knew she needed to have a conversation with Josh to offer a heartfelt apology. She was determined to make things right.

CHAPTER TWENTY-ONE

The next day Kristen returned to work. She had been up since the early hours, diligently tending to her morning tasks. She'd prepared the scones for the day, ensuring that Annabelle was well-equipped to manage the store for a short time, and then promptly set off to pick up her parents from the hotel and take them to the airport. Their conversations had been a blend of encouragement and concern, leaving Kristen with a medley of mixed emotions.

Now, having said goodbye to her parents, she was back at the store again. As she stood behind the counter, her fingers gently tracing the edges of a book cover, Kristen's thoughts were a maze of uncertainties. Her parents had acknowledged her passion for the bookstore, the love she poured into her work, and the potential she had to succeed as a business owner. But the obstacle remained—their decision to release the funds from her trust rested on her ability to secure a suitable location for her venture.

Her heart was torn. After eight years, Moscow was her home, a place she loved and felt connected to. And then there was Josh. She wanted to think they had a future together, but his future was in Moscow. The truth remained that Mary's bookstore already thrived here, and Kristen had no desire to compete with her mentor and friend. It was a conundrum she had yet to unravel, a puzzle with no easy solution. There were some small farming communities around Moscow, but it would be hard to make a case that any of them were big enough to support a new bookstore. The nearest city of notable size was Spokane, an hour and a half away.

With a determined exhale, Kristen pushed aside her contemplations and made her way downstairs to the small office. Bills awaited her attention and she needed to check her emails. With the gentle hum of the air conditioner filling the room, she settled into the office chair and tapped on the keyboard as her mind focused on the mundane tasks at hand.

A soft beep indicated the presence of voicemails, and Kristen's heart skipped a beat when she saw that it was from Mary. She felt anticipation and a flutter of excitement rush through her. Mary's return was imminent, and the thought filled her with both relief and uncertainty.

"Hey Kristen, it's Mary. Just wanted to let you know that I'll be back next week. I hope things have been going well at the store. Can't wait to catch up and hear all about what's been happening. Talk to you soon!"

The message ended, and Kristen sat back in her chair. Changes were coming, whether or not she was ready. Mary's return marked a new chapter—a turning point—that left Kristen grappling with the decisions she needed to make.

On the positive side, no longer being in charge meant the possibility of taking a day off with Josh. They could go river rafting together before the summer was over and she could take him to Seattle to properly meet her parents.

Kristen rose from her seat and made her way upstairs. Anabelle was getting ready to host another story hour and was setting out carpet squares in a semi-circle in the children's area.

"Hey, Annabelle, I'm done working in the office, so I'll handle the front counter, and Josh will be arriving any minute now to take care of the coffee bar. I imagine you'll have a lot of kids today. Word has gotten out about your story hour. You're doing such a great job with it!"

Annabelle smiled in response. "Thank you. If it's okay, I'd like to continue with it after school starts in the fall. Although, it would probably have to be moved to Saturdays."

"You'll need to talk to Mary about that. She'll be back next week."

"Oh, really? That's great. But I hope that doesn't mean you'll be leaving …."

Just then, Josh walked into the store, and a customer appeared near the register, so Kristen used the distractions to avoid responding to Annabelle's comment. She made her way to help the customer and gave Josh a quick greeting in passing. There was something different about his demeanor today, a guardedness that hadn't been present before.

Soon, the shop filled with the sound of animated children, their laughter creating a lively symphony within its homey confines. Kristen's eyes swept over the scene, taking in the sight of mothers chatting at the coffee bar while their little ones sat engrossed in Annabelle's storytelling.

Amidst the flurry of activity, Kristen stood behind the counter, ringing up orders. She glanced toward Josh, his focus unwavering as he expertly filled cup after cup of specialized coffee orders. Her heart sank as she remembered the events of the previous day, her regret amplified by Josh's distant demeanor. A pang of guilt surged within her and she once again determined to make amends with him.

As the last story came to a close and the café eased into a lull, Kristen grabbed a rag and approached Josh, her voice gentle but sincere. "Hey, Josh, can we talk for a moment?"

Josh glanced at her, his gaze questioning, but then another customer approached, and he was busy once again. "Sure, I'll find you when I'm done here."

Kristen nodded, biting her lip as she returned to the front counter. The minutes ticked by, each moment feeling longer than the last until the café finally emptied, the room echoing with newfound quietness.

With a sigh, Josh turned off the coffee machine, his eyes meeting Kristen's as he approached her. "Alright, what's on your mind?"

Kristen's heart fluttered as she met his gaze, the weight of her regret and apology suddenly becoming all too real. "Josh, I'm so sorry about yesterday. I didn't mean to hurt you by not properly introducing you to my parents. I should have been straight about who you are to me, and I regret it deeply."

Josh's expression softened, the wall he had put up beginning to crumble. "It's not just about the introduction, Kristen. It's about us ... where we stand. I've been left hanging, unsure of what we are."

She nodded. Her voice was barely a whisper. "I understand. I've been confused, too. But I want to make it right. I told my parents about you ... about us."

A flicker of surprise danced across Josh's features. His eyes widened slightly, and a small smile tugged at his lips. "Oh?"

Kristen nodded, a warmth spreading through her chest as she continued, "And I want to talk about us, about our future. Mary is coming back next week, and things will be different here. Can we do that? Maybe after work? I thought we could make a picnic dinner and head to the park."

"Yeah, that sounds good, Kristen. Let's do that."

CHAPTER TWENTY-TWO

As dusk began to settle, the park was enveloped in a tranquil twilight glow. Kristen perched on a picnic blanket, a bag of Subway sandwiches resting beside her, her eyes trained on the path leading to the park entrance. A blend of anticipation and contentment fluttered within her, fueled by Josh's imminent arrival.

As if on cue, Josh appeared on the path, his familiar figure approaching with a casual grace. A smile spread across Kristen's face as he drew near, and she waved to him. "Hey there!"

Josh's face lit up with a matching smile, and he joined her on the blanket. "Hey. You know, I was getting pretty hungry. Thanks for picking up these sandwiches."

Kristen handed him one. "No problem. I wish I could have brought something homemade, but I was running late. I needed to get a deposit ready and drop it off at the bank."

They settled into easy conversation, talking about their day and sharing bites of their sandwiches. Josh mentioned his excitement about wrapping up his summer courses, a sense of accomplishment radiating from him.

"I can't believe summer is almost over," Kristen remarked, taking a sip of her drink. "It feels like it just started."

Josh nodded in agreement. "Tell me about it. I've been looking forward to the river rafting trip we talked about. It would be a great way to end the summer."

Kristen smiled, her eyes lighting up. "I think I might be able to swing some time off once Mary returns next week. It'll be good to have her back."

Josh looked thoughtful, "It's weird that I've worked at her store for a few months now and haven't even met her. What's she like?"

Kristen's expression softened, and she spoke with fondness, "You'll like her. She's super smart, she's probably read more books than anyone I've ever known, and she's funny, too. Mary's been like a mentor to me ever since I started working part-time at the shop while in my undergrad years. I honestly don't know what I would have done without her guidance."

He nodded, genuinely intrigued. "You make it look easy, but running the shop on your own must be overwhelming at times."

Kristen leaned back, her gaze drifting to the darkening sky. "It was at first. But the more I did it, the more I realized how much I love it. It just feels right, you know?"

They both fell silent for a moment as Kristen traced circles on the blanket, hesitant to voice what was on her mind.

Finally, Josh broke the silence. "Kristen, you invited me here to talk about us and our future, and ... there's something I've been wanting to tell you."

Her heart skipped a beat, and she turned her attention fully to him. "What is it?"

He met her gaze with a mixture of vulnerability and determination. "I've known this for a while, but I've been hesitant to say it. I've never felt like this about anyone before ...." He paused and leaned closer toward her. "I love you."

The words hung in the air, charged with a mix of emotions. Kristen felt her heart swell with a sweet mixture of joy and bittersweet longing. This was what she had hoped for, yet the timing couldn't have been more complex.

Tears welled up in her eyes as she met his gaze, her voice trembling. "I love you too, Josh."

He offered her a soft smile, his hand finding hers. "I want you to know that I don't want to hold you back from anything. But I'd be lying if I said I wouldn't miss you if you decide to leave."

Kristen's throat tightened, and she squeezed his hand gently. "Josh, you're not holding me back. This is just something I need to figure out. And whatever happens, I want you to be a part of my life."

They sat in silence for a moment as they contemplated their uncertain future. Finally, Kristen took a deep breath and stood. "How about we continue this discussion over some ice cream?"

A playful grin tugged at the corners of Josh's lips. "I like the sound of that."

Hand in hand, they packed up their picnic, made their way to their cars, and drove to Dairy Queen. As they discussed the complexities of their future over Blizzards, Kristen's mind was a whirlwind of thoughts and emotions that fluctuated between uncertainty and hope.

She looked at Josh, her gaze searching. "You know, if I can't find a way to stay near Moscow, I might have to move back to Seattle. It's where my parents are, and I feel like it would make them happy. And then there's my sister, who wants me to move to New York ... but I think I've crossed that possibility off my list. I just need to tell her."

Josh's steady presence comforted her, his fingers lacing through hers. "Kristen, I know you well enough to see how much you've wrestled with these decisions. But you don't have to carry the weight of your family's expectations as your own. You've accomplished so much already; you don't give yourself enough credit."

A wistful smile tugged at the corners of Kristen's lips. "I can't help but feel like I've let them down. I mean, after all the money that was spent for my education ... the gap years ... and now I'm thinking of opening a bookstore and bakery. It's not exactly what they had in mind."

Josh's eyes held a gentle understanding. "Your worth doesn't come from what you accomplish, Kristen. You're loved by God regardless of what path you choose. You don't have to prove anything to anyone. From what you've told me, your parents are good people. I think your parents will love you no matter what."

Tears welled up in Kristen's eyes as she looked at Josh, her heart touched by his unwavering support. She nodded. "Thank you, Josh. I needed to hear that."

As they sat at the small table, the soft hum of conversation around them, Kristen couldn't help but feel a sense of peace settling over her. She glanced at Josh, her heart full. "You know, there's something we can do about all this uncertainty."

He raised an eyebrow, a smile playing on his lips. "What's that?"

She reached for his hand across the table, her voice sincere. "We can pray. We can trust that God has a plan for both of us ... no matter where we end up."

Josh's gaze was warm and steady. "You're right. I've been learning to trust God more, too. We don't have to have all the answers right now."

Kristen felt a sense of relief wash over her. The weight of the future was still there, but it felt a little lighter, a little less daunting. They didn't have all the answers, but they had each other and their faith to guide them.

As they finished their ice cream and walked to their cars, Kristen looped her arm through Josh's, their steps in sync, and their hearts united in a shared commitment to face the future by trusting in God's plan.

CHAPTER TWENTY-THREE

The city was still cloaked in the hush of the pre-dawn hour as Kristen stepped onto the street and walked to the bookstore. Today marked Mary's much-awaited return, and Kristen, unable to suppress the blend of anticipation and apprehension stirring within her, was determined to create a flawless welcome.

In her arms, she carried Lavender, snug in her carrier. It was a regular part of her routine, bringing the cat to and from the bookstore. Kristen had come to enjoy having Lavender as a sort of "roommate," even if she occasionally caused trouble.

As Kristen entered the bookstore, she couldn't shake a tinge of sadness at the thought of Lavender being reunited with Mary, her rightful owner. At least Kristen would only be alone in the apartment for a few days since Sarah was returning from Australia next week. She couldn't wait to see her.

Thinking Mary was still asleep upstairs in her apartment, Kristen went to the basement kitchen. Soon, the comforting scent of scones filled the room as she started a fresh batch. She also thought of *Mrs. Canfield's Cookery Book for the Modern Woman*, which she had tucked securely in her bag that morning. Returning it to Mary felt like parting with an old friend. It had been a source of comfort and inspiration, a kind of stand-in for Mary while she managed the bookstore alone.

As Kristen worked in the kitchen, she thought about the changes before her. Mary's trust in her abilities had been a gift, and though Kristen still wasn't sure what her future held, she finally had some clarity about what she wanted. She thought of Josh, then offered a silent prayer that God would provide a way for them to stay together.

Just as she was pulling the first tray of scones from the oven, the door to the kitchen swung open and there stood Mary, a fond smile gracing her lips. In her arms, she cradled Lavender, who blinked contentedly.

Kristen rushed forward to embrace her boss and friend. "Mary! Oh, it's wonderful to have you back!"

Mary's hug was warm and reassuring, much like the return of a long-lost family member. "Kristen, the store looks absolutely magnificent. Your touch during my absence is unmistakable."

Kristen's heart swelled with pride and relief. She had put her heart and soul into managing the store during Mary's absence, and the reassurance from her mentor was exactly what she needed to hear. And when Mary sampled one of the scones and praised her baking skills, Kristen felt a surge of happiness.

Over cups of coffee, Mary spoke of her sister's improving health, and Kristen recounted some of her daily trials and joys while managing the bookstore. Before they knew it, it was time to open the shop. It was a bittersweet reunion, knowing that it meant handing back over some of the responsibilities she'd cherished. Yet Mary's return brought a sense of wholeness to the shop.

Kristen couldn't help but feel a profound sense of gratitude. She loved this time of day, right before opening, and Kristen looked forward to introducing Mary to Josh and Sasha. Kristen knew it was important to tell Mary about her relationship with Josh and wondered how Mary would react. Hopefully, she'd approve. "You'll get to meet both of our new employees today, Mary. Sasha and Josh will be in soon."

Mary stood and headed up the stairs, "Oh, good, I'm excited to meet them! We have lots to discuss later, including getting you some vacation time before the summer ends. You certainly deserve it."

Kristen felt a lightness in her step as she followed Mary up to the shop. She couldn't wait to tell Josh they could start planning their rafting adventure together.

The shop was soon a whirlwind of activity. As soon as they opened the front doors, customers began pouring in, ready to shop or just visit with friends over coffee. Cries of delight punctuated the air as some of the regulars realized Mary was back. Kristen couldn't help but smile when she overheard one lady say to her boss, "I sure missed you, Mary, and I'm glad you're back, but you should know you have a treasure with your girl, Kristen. She took care of this place as if it were her own!"

Kristen introduced Mary to Sasha and Josh when they arrived, and Mary immediately put them at ease with her enthusiastic hugs and welcoming manner. It was evident that the camaraderie amongst the staff would stay as strong as ever. But amidst the hectic morning, there wasn't time for any of them to chat for long.

During a lull in customers, Mary looked at the clock and asked Kristen to join her for lunch. Kristen accepted her offer, welcoming the opportunity to have a long-awaited conversation with her mentor and boss.

Mary led the way upstairs to her apartment. She explained that she hadn't had time to restock her kitchen since returning the night before, so she'd ordered some burritos. The aroma of savory spices filled the apartment as they settled in at the small dining table.

Before joining Mary, Kristen went downstairs to retrieve *Mrs. Canfield's Cookery Book* from her bag. She wanted to show Mary the treasures she had discovered within its pages and the recipe for the scones that had been such a hit with their customers. But when Kristen reached into her bag, her fingers met empty space where the book should have been. Panic fluttered briefly in her chest before she reasoned that she must have inadvertently left it at home.

She joined Mary in her upstairs apartment and, while accepting a burrito Mary had ordered, Kristen mentioned the cookbook, promising to bring it the next day. Mary was gracious, assuring her that it was no problem.

As they ate and chatted, it was decided that Kristen would be granted a week off, beginning in two days. This would ensure that she would be back in time before school resumed for the fall semester. At that point, Sasha could only work occasional Saturdays, and Josh would have to reduce his work hours to accommodate his full-time college course load.

With a warm smile, Mary thanked Kristen for the information and expressed her appreciation for how the store had been managed in her absence.

Kristen took a deep breath, "I have something else to tell you. Josh and I are seeing each other."

"Seeing each other?" Mary's face registered confusion. "Of course, you're seeing each other. You work together."

"No, I mean we're dating."

"Oh? Well, that's wonderful, dear! He seems like a good man."

"You don't mind?"

"Mind? Why would I mind?"

"Well, because I hired him, and then I was his boss, and ... well, my sister didn't think it was a good idea at first ...."

Mary laughed and waved her hand as if shooing the rest of Kristen's words away. "Good heavens! You know me, dear. I've never been much of a stickler for the 'rules,' per se. If you're happy, I'm happy."

Kristen relaxed into her chair. "Thank you," she smiled. "I'm very happy."

Their conversation then turned to the book club meeting that was scheduled for the following day. Mary assured Kristen that they were still more than welcome to gather in her apartment and even hinted that she might join them if the shop wasn't too busy.

As they finished their lunch, Kristen decided to write down the scone recipe for Mary since she had it memorized by that point. She wanted her boss to have it readily available.

Returning downstairs, Kristen couldn't help but feel a sense of relief and anticipation even though she still hadn't brought up the idea of opening a store of her own to Mary. Maybe after a few days away from the store, she would have a greater perspective and an answer to her prayers. It would be better to wait until then.

CHAPTER TWENTY-FOUR

"Flight 277, Seattle to New York, is now boarding group B," the voice over the intercom announced.

Kristen stood and picked up her bag, ready for part one of her vacation—a few days with Amy in Manhattan. When she returned, part two would include a day of whitewater rafting with Josh and their friends.

The flight was long but uneventful, and Kristen spent most of it sleeping. Somewhat rested by the time they landed, she made her way outside to the pick-up area. She scanned the crowd for Amy, spotting her sister's familiar face at a distance.

"Amy!" Kristen exclaimed as she rushed into her sister's arms. After a long embrace, they got into a waiting cab and began to catch up on all they had missed since their last visit.

Amy's apartment was a charming studio in a historic brownstone building near the financial district. Kristen loved how Amy decorated it with personal touches that reflected her sister's vibrant personality.

Over the next few days, Kristen and Amy explored the city together, visiting their favorite spots and discovering new ones. They strolled through Central Park, admired the art at the Metropolitan Museum of Art, and caught a Broadway show.

One evening, while sharing a delicious meal at a bustling Italian restaurant, Kristen opened up to Amy about her relationship with Josh. She told her about their upcoming rafting trip, their shared love of literature, and how he made her feel.

"I'm so happy for you, Kristen," Amy said, her eyes sparkling. "Josh sounds like a wonderful guy."

Kristen smiled and took a bite of pasta, feeling a twinge of gratitude and longing. She was so grateful for her sister's support, and she missed Josh with an ache in her heart that she hadn't expected. It had only been three days since she'd seen him last. "There's something else I need to tell you."

Amy took a sip of wine. "I knew it. Tell me."

Kristen took a deep breath, setting her fork down for a moment as she gathered her thoughts. "I've been thinking a lot this summer about what I really want in life. And, well, I've decided that I want to open my own bookstore and bakery."

Amy's eyes lit up with excitement. "Wow, Kristen! That's amazing! I can totally see you running a place like that. Huh, you really enjoyed working at Mary's bookshop that much?"

Kristen nodded and smiled, "Yes, it's not without some challenges, but it's so rewarding."

Amy nodded, her smile widening. "I love it! That's such a wonderful idea. Have you thought about where you want to open it?"

"Yeah," Kristen replied. "Mom thinks I should open a bookstore in Seattle, but I want to stay near Moscow. I love the community there, and it just feels like the right place for me. And then, there's Josh...."

Amy reached across the table and squeezed Kristen's hand. "It's that serious, huh?"

"I'm not sure how serious it is with Josh. It's still early, but I do love him." She paused. "But there's something else I'm working through, too. I don't want to open a bookstore in direct competition with Mary's. I respect what she's built, and I don't want to take away from that."

Amy's eyes softened with understanding. "That's thoughtful of you, Kristen. Have you talked to Mary about it? She might have some insights or even be supportive of your idea."

"I haven't talked to her yet," Kristen admitted. "But I want to make sure it's something that won't impede on her business. I'm proud of you, sis. Following your dreams and being considerate of others—that's the Kristen I know and love. You'll figure it out."

"Thank you, Amy. Your support means the world to me."

As Kristen's visit drew to a close, she started to feel a pang of sadness. She loved spending time with Amy and exploring the city she used to dream of living in. But she couldn't deny that she missed Josh terribly.

On the flight back to Moscow, Kristen reflected on her sister's words. Although she loved visiting New York, she was eager to return to her small town in Idaho.

Despite her late-night arrival, Josh was waiting for her at the airport. When he wrapped his arms around her, she knew she was exactly where she was meant to be.

When they arrived at her apartment, it was after midnight. As soon as Josh parked the car, he leaned across to kiss Kristen, lingering for a long while. Neither of them wanted to say goodbye again so soon, but it was late. Reluctantly, Josh pulled away and held her gaze.

"I'll go to the store tomorrow and get some snacks for our day on the river," Kristen said, kissing him again before unbuckling her seatbelt. "Are you sure there isn't anything else I can contribute?"

Josh shook his head, "Nope, we're all set." He got out of the car, pulled her suitcase from the trunk, and carried it to her front door. "Get some rest. I'll call you tomorrow. After school and work, I'll need to load up the rafting gear, so I'm not sure if we'll have time to get together."

"No problem; I understand. Thank you for picking me up so late. I missed you."

Josh smiled, "Of course—happy to do it. I missed you too."

When Kristen entered, the apartment was dark except for one lamp in the hallway. Immediately, she noticed Sarah's pile of luggage in the living room, and quietly, she set her own bag down. Kristen smiled, happy to have her roommate back from Australia. It felt good to have someone at home—someone who would leave a light on for her. Kristen tiptoed to her room, not wanting to disturb Sarah's sleep. There would be plenty of stories to share in the morning.

Lying in bed, Kristen thought about the whirlwind of the past few days: the vibrant streets of New York, her heartfelt conversations with Amy, and her longing for Josh. It was a mix of emotions, but as she closed her eyes, she focused on the warmth she felt when Josh picked her up at the airport.

Kristen awoke to the smell of coffee brewing. She followed the aroma to the kitchen, where she found Sarah making breakfast.

"Good morning! How was your trip?" Sarah asked, giving Kristen a tight morning hug.

"It was amazing. New York is always a blast, and spending time with Amy was just what I needed," Kristen replied, a smile playing on her lips. "And how was *your* trip?"

"Fabulous! I brought you something … a souvenir." Sarah smiled and handed Kristen a plate of toast.

"You brought back toast with jam?"

Sarah shook her head. "Vegemite. I ate it all the time when I was in Australia. Now I can't live without it. Try it!"

Kristen took a bite. Though it was hard to describe, she liked the strong, salty flavor.

Over breakfast, Kristen shared the details of her adventures in the city with her sister, her idea to open a bookstore, and, of course, Josh. Sarah, in turn, regaled Kristen with stories of her time in Australia and the exciting experiences she had.

The day passed quickly, filled with laughter, shared memories, and lots of laundry. As promised, Josh called Kristen, and they ironed out the details for the following day's rafting trip. Kristen and Sarah decided to spend the evening watching movies, a perfect way to unwind after their recent days of travel.

CHAPTER TWENTY-FIVE

A palpable buzz of anticipation filled the air as Kristen, Josh, Sarah, Todd, and Leah exited the outfitter's van at the river brink in Orofino. Their long-awaited day of adventure on the Clearwater River was about to commence.

With the confidence of a seasoned rafter, Josh reassured them that the trip promised a leisurely float perfect for beginners rather than a pulse-pounding white-water experience. Kristen, while excited, felt a flutter of nerves in her stomach.

As they unloaded the raft, inflating it to its full glory, their laughter and banter mingled with the rustling leaves and the gentle lapping of the river.

Sarah regaled them with tales of kangaroos and coral reefs, her eyes sparkling with contagious excitement. Kristen was pleased that she could join them on the river. It was a perfect opportunity to reconnect, relax, and introduce two of the most important people in her life to each other: her best friend and her boyfriend. She hoped they hit it off. So far, it seemed to be going well.

With the raft prepped and their life jackets secured, they pushed off from the riverbank. The water carried them smoothly, and the sun warmed their faces. Kristen felt safe with Josh, and she couldn't help but marvel at the beauty of the surroundings. Towering trees lined the banks, and the occasional glimpse of wildlife added to the enchantment—a deer sipping from the water's edge, a playful family of otters frolicking on the beach, and majestic eagles soaring overhead.

As they floated along, the worries that had tugged at Kristen's mind seemed to drift away with the current. She'd made a conscious effort to set aside thoughts of her uncertain future, at least for this day. The company of good friends and the allure of the outdoors had an undeniable way of soothing the soul.

The river meandered gracefully through the landscape, and their gentle paddling kept the raft on course. Todd and Josh shared stories of their previous rafting escapades, and the group chuckled at their wild tales. It felt like a carefree escape from reality, a chance to live fully in the present.

At one particularly spirited bend, their raft hit a submerged rock. In an instant, it tipped, sending everyone into the chilly embrace of the river. Laughter and splashes filled the air as they scrambled back aboard, their drenched clothes clinging to them.

With the raft righted and everyone safely back inside it, they continued their journey. As the day progressed, their camaraderie deepened. They shared sandwiches and stories, dipped their toes in the water, and basked in the beauty of the Idaho wilderness.

By the time they reached their destination at the confluence of the Clearwater and Snake Rivers near Lewiston, the sun hung low on the horizon, casting long shadows across the water. Exhausted but happy, they piled into Todd's Suburban, which Leah and Todd had left there the night before so they'd have a ride home.

As they made the forty-minute drive back to Moscow, Kristen's eyelids grew heavy as she sat in the third-row seat beside a pile of oars and helmets. She reflected on their fun adventures on the river and looked forward to the following day. She and Josh both had one more day off from work to spend together, which was definitely something she could get used to. She loved spending time with him. She knew the uncertainties of her future still loomed, but for now, she had learned the art of letting go, savoring the present, and trusting that God would carry her where she needed to go.

The slowing of the van as they pulled into town caused Kristen to open her eyes. "This was the first summer I didn't work out on the river with my dad in ten years," she overheard Josh saying to Todd. "I had to take a couple of extra classes this summer so I would have enough credits to graduate this winter. Today made me realize how much I've missed it."

Todd made a left turn onto Kristen and Sarah's street. "Yeah, today was awesome. We're lucky to live here. I wouldn't want to live anywhere else."

"Me either."

A hitch in Kristen's breath betrayed the emotions churning within her. She'd seen how happy in his element Josh was on the river. It had been evident that was where he belonged. It made her reflect on her own aspirations. Was it possible for their dreams to meld together and for both to still be happy? Or were they being led to separate paths?

***

"It Is You" by the Newsboys played on the stereo as Kristen pulled up in front of Josh's house. She'd been listening to the song on repeat lately. It usually brightened her spirits, but today, she felt a certain heaviness in her chest, the weight of the thoughts that had haunted her since the rafting trip. She loved Josh deeply, and being with him brought her immense happiness. Yet, she couldn't shake the fear that their dreams might lead them in different directions.

Josh climbed into the car, offering her a warm smile. Sensing that something was amiss, his smile dimmed. "What's wrong?"

Kristen hesitated for a moment. "It's just ... I've been thinking about us, Josh," her voice a whisper of uncertainty. ". Our dreams, our futures. It seems like such a challenge to make everything work if we stay together. I don't want to hold you back."

Josh reached over and gently squeezed her hand. "Kristen, we'll figure it out," he said with a reassuring smile. "We're a team, right?"

She nodded; her heart warmed by his words. "Yes, we are."

They shared a moment of quiet reflection, the weight of unspoken thoughts lingering in the air.

When they reached Orofino, Josh got into his family's outfitter van and Kristen followed him back to Moscow. Alone with her thoughts, Kristen offered up a silent prayer, a plea for guidance and clarity, hoping that somehow, she and Josh would find a way to align their aspirations without sacrificing their love for each other.

Later that evening, Kristen was filled with nervous excitement as she prepared to meet Josh's parents for dinner. Looking at her reflection in the mirror one more time, her fingers traced the soft fabric of her favorite dress, which she had selected to exude elegance and confidence,

When Josh picked her up at her apartment, he sensed her apprehension. He offered her a reassuring smile and gently held her hand as they drove to his parents' house. His calm demeanor was a soothing balm to her jittery nerves.

As they stepped onto the porch, the warm glow of the house seemed to beckon them inside. With a nod of encouragement, Josh ushered her through the front door, calling out to announce their arrival.

The aroma of rosemary-roasted chicken and garlic mashed potatoes filled the air as Josh and Kristen entered the tastefully appointed dining room. Jeff and Claire Brooks greeted them with genuine warmth, their smiles reaching their eyes.

"Kristen! It's so lovely to finally meet you," Josh's father exclaimed, enveloping Kristen in a hug that smelled faintly of cedar. "Josh has talked so much about you."

Throughout dinner, she was charmed by Josh's family, feeling a sense of belonging and warmth in their presence. But even amidst the laughter and camaraderie, Kristen's internal struggle remained. She couldn't deny that her love for Josh was intertwined with a growing realization that it would be wrong to ask him to relocate to Seattle. But how could she remain in Moscow? It didn't seem possible.

CHAPTER TWENTY-SIX

The small bell above the bookstore's door rang as Kristen stepped inside, her mind racing with thoughts of the missing cookbook. She had scoured her apartment and every nook and cranny of the store, but it had simply vanished. A sense of loss tugged at her heart, an unexpected ache for a book that had been a quiet companion through the ups and downs of her life over the past summer.

Mary, who had been arranging some new arrivals on a shelf, looked up as Kristen entered and greeted her with a welcoming smile. "Good morning! Boy, am I glad you're back. It has been busy around here. Did you enjoy your time off?"

Kristen nodded her head, a feeling of guilt settling in. "I did. It was a mix of rest and adventure, just what I needed ...." She paused. "Mary, I've looked everywhere for that cookbook of yours that I borrowed but I can't find it. Losing that book feels like losing a friend. I'm so sorry; I feel awful. I'm worried that it might have accidentally have been sold. If I left it out...it almost happened once before..."

Mary chuckled, setting aside the book she was holding. "Oh, don't worry about it, Kristen. I honestly can't even remember the book. But if it ever turns up, I'll make sure you get it back. It's all yours. It's obviously got a special place in your heart. Believe me, I understand how books can be like friends. Antoine de Saint-Exupery said, 'The tender friendship one gives up on parting, leave their bite on the heart, but also a curious feeling of a treasure somewhere buried.'"

Kristen appreciated Mary's understanding and nodded gratefully.

"Actually, Kristen, I have something to share with you as well. This past week has confirmed something that's been on my mind. It's time for me to retire," Mary admitted, her eyes gazing out into the cozy confines of the bookstore she had lovingly cultivated over the years.

Kristen's brows furrowed in surprise. "Retire? But, Mary, you are the heart and soul of this place. You can't just leave it."

Mary smiled warmly at Kristen's concern. "Well, I've been thinking that if I retire, perhaps I could sell the store. And that's where you come in. What are your future plans, Kristen? Would you be interested in the store or are you still planning on moving to New York or Seattle?"

Kristen hesitated for a moment, her excitement was building. She took a deep breath, realizing that this conversation was as much about her future as it was about Mary's.

" Actually, I've been thinking about opening a bookstore of my own," Kristen confessed, her voice soft but resolute. "But I didn't want to be in competition with you, so I thought I might have to leave. However, I really want to stay in Moscow. I love this town, Mary, and I don't want to leave it. Taking over your store would allow me to be part of the community, run my own place, and make a difference."

Mary nodded, a thoughtful look on her face. "That's wonderful, Kristen. I can't think of a better person to continue the legacy of this store. Take some time to think about it and let's keep this conversation going. We'll both need to figure out the financial side of things, but I'm sure we can figure something out that works for both of us."

As Kristen headed downstairs to make the scones, she couldn't help but thank God for hearing her prayers. He was nudging her toward the very opportunity she had hoped for—to stay in Moscow and pursue her dream.

***

Kristen returned to the bookstore after her lunch break with a lightness in her step and a sense of hope in her heart. She'd walked to the park, using the time to make a phone call, and the conversation with her mom had gone even better than she could have hoped. As she settled back into her work, her mind raced with the possibilities that lay ahead.

After a few hours passed, Kristen couldn't contain her excitement any longer. She needed to share the news with Josh, whose unwavering support had been a constant source of strength. She took a break from entering inventory into the computer and picked up her phone. Her heart raced as she waited for him to answer.

"Hey, Kristen," Josh's warm voice greeted her.

"Hey," she replied, unable to contain her enthusiasm. I've got some incredible news to share."

Josh laughed softly. "You sound excited. What's up?"

Taking a deep breath to calm her racing thoughts, Kristen began to share how Mary's unexpected retirement and offer to sell the store would allow her to stay in Moscow, be part of the community, and run her own place. Mary would continue to serve as her mentor, and her parents were flying in to meet with Kristen, Mary, and a lawyer. As she paused for a reaction, Kristen could hear the smile in Josh's voice as he responded. "That's amazing, Kristen. I'm really happy for you—for both of us. I've always wanted want you to stay here and it sounds like everything is falling into place for that to happen."

Kristen felt a profound sense of gratitude wash over her. "It does feel that way. But I'm also aware that there's a long road ahead, and a lot of details to work out."

Josh's voice was filled with reassurance. "You'll tackle those details as they come, Kristen. And remember, you've got a lot of people who believe in you, and I'm right here by your side."

Her heart swelled with affection for Josh and her parents, who had both been pillars of strength during this time of transition. Kristen couldn't help but feel that she was on the right path, guided not only by her own dreams but also by the support and faith of those who loved her and, most of all, by God above.

As she hung up the phone, she closed her eyes for a moment and offered a silent prayer of gratitude. She thanked God for the opportunities lying ahead of her and asked for wisdom and strength to navigate the journey.

***

The following days brought a whirlwind of activity as Kristen and Mary delved deeper into the logistics of the bookstore transition. The sweet little space seemed to be bubbling with anticipation. Kristen also found herself spending more time with Josh, discussing their own plans, dreams, and the intricate details that awaited them.

One evening, as the sun dipped below the horizon, Kristen and Josh sat on the steps of the bookstore, admiring the warm hues of the sunset. "I can't believe how everything is falling into place," Kristen mused, her eyes reflecting the joy and excitement bubbling within her.

Josh smiled, turning his gaze to Kristen. "It's like a dream, isn't it? I love seeing you so happy and driven. This bookstore seems to be more than just a business venture for you."

Kristen nodded, a soft laugh escaping her lips. "It *is* more than a business, Josh. It's about creating a place where people can connect with each other through books. And you know what makes it even better? Having you by my side through all of this."

Josh reached for Kristen's hand, intertwining his fingers with hers. "I wouldn't be anywhere else. I've always believed in you and your dreams. And this ... this feels like it's a part of God's plan, like we're building something beautiful together."

As they sat in companionable silence, continuing to watch the sky change colors, Kristen felt a profound sense of gratitude for Josh's unwavering support. Their transition from friends to something more had been a natural evolution of their deep connection. Now, as they faced the prospect of embarking on this new chapter together, Kristen couldn't imagine anyone else by her side.

"I have to admit," Josh said, breaking the silence as he turned toward her, "I've been thinking about us a lot lately. With everything happening, it feels like a turning point for both of us."

Kristen turned to him, tilting her head in curiosity. "What do you mean?"

Josh took a deep breath, his gaze holding hers. "I mean, Kristen, that I love you deeply." He smiled softly; his thumb tracing circles on the back of her hand. "I want to spend the rest of my life with you, and I wonder if you feel the same way?" As he awaited her response, he pulled a velvet box out of his pocket and opened it. Inside was a beautiful emerald-cut diamond on a platinum band. "I've been holding on to this for a while .... waiting for the right time."

She looked into Josh's eyes and saw sincerity and affection mirrored in them. A warmth spread through

Kristen's chest, and she felt a surge of emotions. "Josh, I ... Yes! I love you too." Kristen's heart swelled with joy, gratitude, and the fluttering of something more.

Josh leaned in, his lips meeting hers in a sweet, tender kiss. As they pulled away, the small bell above the bookstore's door rang softly, echoing the beginning of a new chapter for both the bookstore and their relationship. In that moment, Kristen felt a deep sense of contentment, knowing that she didn't have to do anything but rest in this beautiful life that God had for her.

CHAPTER TWENTY-SEVEN

Kristen's heart swelled with pride and joy as she watched Josh walk across the stage to receive his diploma from the University of Idaho. The Kibbie Dome erupted in cheers and applause, and Kristen stood and clapped as he walked off the stage, his smile radiant.

As Kristen sat down, she couldn't help but reflect on the whirlwind of changes that had transformed her life over the past six months. At her own graduation, Kristen had been filled with uncertainty about her future. She hadn't even thought of opening her own bookstore in Moscow, and the idea of finding romantic love was nothing more than a fantasy. But God had opened her eyes and planted new desires in her heart to pursue the gifts he'd placed right before her.

The path to realizing these dreams had been fraught with challenges, but she'd never been alone. Now, she was the proud owner of Mary's Bookshop, and it would continue to be a cherished part of the community. Mary, who still lived above the store with Lavender, ultimately decided to only semi-retire, taking on all the baking duties so Kristen could focus on everything else.

As Kristen gazed at the sparkling diamond engagement ring on her finger, a symbol of the love and commitment she shared with Josh, her heart swelled even more. Josh was not only graduating from college, but was also taking on more responsibilities with his family's rafting business. He'd also signed a contract with a publishing company for his recently completed novel, a testament to his determination and talent.

Kristen couldn't have been prouder of her fiancé. She admired his dedication to his passions and his unwavering support of her dreams. She couldn't help but think about how unexpected and beautiful their journey had been so far, and she looked forward to building a life together that was filled with love, adventure, and the pursuit of their individual and shared goals.

***

The graduation party at Josh's parents' house was a joyful affair. Friends and family had gathered to celebrate Josh's achievement, and the atmosphere was filled with laughter and warmth. Kristen's parents had even made the journey from Seattle to join in the festivities. Kristen couldn't help but feel grateful for the close bond growing between their two families.

Amidst the lively conversations and laughter, Kristen's parents stood with Kristen and Josh around a small table on the patio, surrounded by the glow of string lights.

Kristen's mother spoke with a smile, "You two have accomplished so much. Josh, in addition to your graduation, your mother just told me about your new book contract. And Kristen, we're so proud of you with the bookstore."

Her father added, "And with the wedding just around the corner in June, it's like watching a beautiful story unfold. You're creating a life together that's truly remarkable."

Kristen and Josh exchanged a loving glance, their hearts full of gratitude for the support of their families. Kristen's mother hugged her tightly, whispering, "You've found a wonderful partner, Kristen. We're so happy for you both."

Josh shook hands with Kristen's father, a genuine smile on his face. "Thank you for everything. We're excited for what the future holds."

As the evening wore on and the party began to wind down, Kristen and Josh found a quiet moment to slip away. They retreated to Josh's cozy casita behind the main house, where the soft glow of string lights illuminated the room. They settled onto the couch with steaming mugs of hot chocolate, gazing out the window as snowflakes danced in the wintry night.

Josh broke the comfortable silence. "You know, today was amazing. I can't believe I've finally graduated. It took long enough! I'm excited to start a new chapter."

Kristen smiled, and her eyes filled with affection. "Hey, now. You made it two years faster than I did! It took me a long while to figure out what I wanted, but looking back, it seems God was lining up the pieces the whole time, preparing me for where I am today."

Josh's expression grew thoughtful. "Speaking of new chapters, are you going to keep calling your business Mary's Bookshop?"

A mischievous glint appeared in Kristen's eyes. She leaned in closer to Josh, her voice a soft whisper. "Actually, I've got a surprise for you."

Josh raised an eyebrow. "A surprise? What is it?"

"While we were celebrating your graduation today," Kristen said, her smile growing wider, "I had a new sign installed at the store. I thought we could go see it together."

Josh's eyes sparkled with excitement. "Well, don't keep me waiting. Let's go see this surprise of yours!"

They set down their mugs, bundled up in warm coats, and headed out into the crisp winter night. The short drive to the store was filled with anticipation. Kristen asked Josh to park around the corner from the store and once he was out of the car, she instructed him to close his eyes. She led him to the front of the shop, which was bathed in the soft glow of streetlights. She stopped and turned to face him.

"Look up," she instructed.

Josh moved his gaze upward. There, hanging above the door, was a beautiful new sign that read, "Serenity Books." The elegant lettering was illuminated from below, casting a warm and inviting glow onto the snowy sidewalk.

Josh's eyes widened in surprise, and a delighted smile spread across his face. "Serenity Books," he repeated. "It's perfect, Kristen."

She beamed at him. "I'm glad you like it. I wanted the name to reflect how I feel about this place ... and how I want other people to feel when they come through those doors."

Josh took Kristen's hand, "It's more than perfect. It's absolutely you."

As they stood hand in hand, gazing at the sign, the snow continued to fall around them. It was a moment of true serenity and hope, a symbol of the beautiful life they were building together, one chapter at a time.

Dawn Klinge

RECIPES

Chocolate Chip Scones

2 cups all-purpose flour
¼ cup sugar
1 ¼ teaspoon baking powder
¼ teaspoon baking soda
¼ tsp salt
½ cup unsalted butter, cold
1 cup dark chocolate chips
¾ cup buttermilk
1 tsp vanilla extract

Instructions
- Preheat oven to 400°F. Whisk together flour, sugar, baking powder, baking soda, and salt in a large bowl.
- Grate the cold butter using a cheese grater. This is an easy way to get it into small pieces to incorporate in the dry ingredients. If you do not have a cheese grater, you can just cut into small cubes. Blend the grated butter in with the flour mixture using a pastry cutter or 2 knives. The mixture should be clumpy and look like course crumbs. Mix in the chocolate chips.
- In a small measuring cup, mix together the buttermilk and vanilla. Mix into the flour mixture until JUST

incorporated. DO NOT over mix, this will make the scones too dense.

- Put a small amount of flour onto a clean surface and knead the dough briefly. Shape the dough into a circle that is about 1 ½ inches thick. Cut the circle in half and then each half into 4-5 wedges (depending on how big you want your scones).
- Put the wedges on a baking sheet covered with parchment paper. Brush the tops with a little bit of milk and then lightly sprinkle with sugar.
- Bake for 20-22 minutes until tops are golden brown and toothpick inserted comes out clean. Cool on a wire rack.

Chicken Pot Pie

1 (3 1/2-lb.) broiler fryer
2 qts. water
1 tsp. salt
1/2 tsp. pepper
1 stalk celery, cut into 2-in. pieces
1 medium onion, quartered
1 bay leaf
1 (16-oz.) package frozen mixed vegetables
2 large potatoes, peeled and cubed
1/2 cup unsalted butter or margarine
1/2 cup all-purpose flour
1 cup milk
1 1/2 tsp. salt
1 1/4 tsp. pepper
1/4 tsp. dried thyme
2 hard-cooked eggs, sliced
1 (9-in.) refrigerated piecrust

Instructions

- Cook chicken: Combine first 7 ingredients in a large Dutch oven; bring to a boil. Cover, reduce heat, and simmer 1 hour or until chicken is tender. Remove chicken, reserving broth in Dutch oven; discard vegetables and bay leaf. Let chicken cool; skin, bone, and cut into bite-size pieces.

- Cook vegetables: With a large spoon, skim fat (oily liquid) from surface of broth reserved in Dutch oven; bring broth to a boil. Add frozen vegetables and potatoes; return to a boil. Reduce heat, cover, and simmer 8 minutes or until tender. Remove vegetables from broth, and set aside. Measure 3 cups broth; set aside. Reserve remaining broth for other uses.

- Make sauce: Melt butter in Dutch oven over low heat; add flour, stirring until smooth. Cook 1 minute, stirring constantly. Gradually add 3 cups broth and milk; cook over medium heat, stirring constantly, until mixture is thickened and bubbly. Stir in 11/2 teaspoons salt, 11/4 teaspoons pepper, and thyme. Add vegetables, chicken, and hard-cooked eggs; stir gently. Spoon into a lightly greased 13- x 9- x 2-inch baking dish; set aside.

- Build and bake pot pie: Roll out piecrust on a lightly floured surface into a 15- x 11-inch rectangle (piecrust will be very thin). Place over chicken mixture; crimp edges, pressing against sides of baking dish. Cut slits in top for steam to escape; bake at 400° for 20 minutes or until golden brown.

Dawn Klinge

ACKNOWLEDGMENTS

This book wouldn't exist without the vision and dedication of others. My deepest gratitude goes to Jenny Knipfer, who not only dreamed up the *Apron Strings* series but also planned, executed, and invited me to be a part of it. Thank you for sharing this creative journey with me.

A heartfelt thank you to Samantha Fury for bringing the story to life with her beautiful cover design and formatting.

To Dalene Bickel, my editor, your keen eye and insightful suggestions helped refine the manuscript and make it shine.

Amanda Waters, my long-time critique partner, your unwavering support and honest feedback have been invaluable throughout this process.

To my family, your love and understanding provided the foundation for this project. Thank you for believing in me and cheering me on.

And lastly, to my readers, your enthusiasm inspires me to keep writing. Thank you for picking up this book and joining me on this adventure.

ABOUT DAWN

Dawn Klinge is an author from Wenatchee, Washington. She's married to her high school sweetheart and has two grown kids. Travel and history inspire her writing. She's currently studying creative writing at Oxford University. Her Historic Hotels Collection includes Sorrento Girl, Palmer Girl, and Biltmore Girl. She enjoys writing contemporary and historical romance novels that feature strong women. She is a member of the American Christian Fiction Writers.

When she's not writing, she loves to read, play golf, ski, or hike. She also loves eating good food but would prefer to leave the cooking to others.

NOVEL PREVIEW

Historic Hotels Collection

Book 1

Sorrento Girl

It's 1938, and Ann Brooks has big dreams for her new life as a Seattle College coed. She's left the old-fashioned ways of her small country town behind to pursue higher education and a teaching career.

But not everyone is ready for change.

Society still preaches that a woman's place is in the home. Some refuse to see Ann as an equal deserving of an education — let alone a career — and Ann's friends think school is simply a springboard to pursue a marriage of wealth and convenience.

When Ann meets Paul, an aspiring journalist with strong ideas of his own, she learns an unexpected lesson in courage and discovers what it really means to live her dreams.

Will Ann give up everything she thought she wanted for love? Or can she have it all?

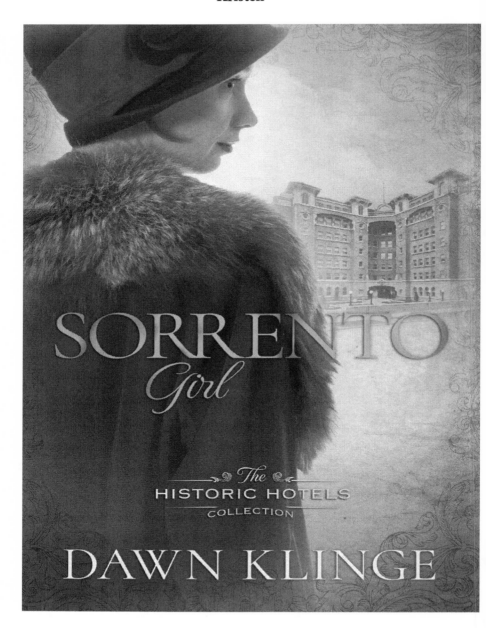

SORRENTO GIRL - CHAPTER ONE

August 15, 1938

King Street Station, Seattle, WA

"Hotel Sorrento, please," Ann said to the taxi driver as she handed him her suitcase. Getting into the back of the cab, she moved aside the newspaper a previous passenger had left behind, placing her handbag on top. She wanted to take her things to the hotel first, find her room, and get some lunch before walking over to her new school for a meeting with Mrs. Prouty, the Dean of Women at Seattle College. The two had first met a year ago when Aunt Rose insisted on introducing Ann to her friend.

"Where are you going to college?" Rose had asked Ann last summer.

"I'm not." Though Ann wanted to continue her education, it wasn't within her reach.

"Why not?"

"I can't afford it." She didn't want to dwell on the disappointment.

Rose, knowing her niece well, hadn't accepted that answer. "Nonsense. You're going to come to Seattle, and I'll help you. We'll figure it out. I think I know just the right place." And figure it out, they did. Ann could hardly believe it. Not only had the money for tuition been provided for through a combination of scholarships and a small inheritance left behind by her maternal grandparents, but she also had a job and a place to live.

She would be working as a mother's helper for a family with four kids, and her new home would be a room at Hotel Sorrento. One wing of the hotel had been temporarily leased as a women's dormitory for the college.

Seattle College was a small Jesuit school on First Hill. A College of Education had recently been established within the school after some controversy over admitting women. It was a fight that had gone all the way to the Vatican. Ann would be among one of the first groups of women to graduate from the new program when she finished. According to Aunt Rose, it was a place for trailblazers.

After being assured that Ann would attend college, Rose took off on a six-month sabbatical from her teaching job at the University of Washington to conduct some research on cathedrals in England. She would be home soon, and Ann was anxious to catch up with her.

The cab lurched along cobbled roads, and the scenery changed from dusty city streets to a quieter, more genteel neighborhood called First Hill. Stately homes with vast green lawns and iron gates lined the road. The Hotel Sorrento came into view. The Italian oasis-style building reached seven stories high. Its red-brick L-shape gracefully curved around a large front driveway and formal garden area. A smartly dressed doorman in a red suit with gold buttons stood attentively near the entrance. Ann said a quiet prayer of gratitude and awe as she took in the building's beauty. "Welcome to Hotel Sorrento, the crown jewel of the Northwest!" said the man as he opened Ann's door.

Inside, the rich mahogany paneled walls, chandeliers, and thick oriental rugs gave the lobby a feeling of warmth and luxury. Ann had never stayed anywhere so lovely before. After she checked in at the front desk, a bellhop escorted her to her new homeroom, 302 in the east wing. Ann entered the room, and her breath caught! The view was striking! Through a large window framed by thick gold-colored drapes, she could see Puget Sound and much of the city.

Kristen

Two twin beds with mahogany headboards and white matelassé coverlets took up most of the space in the simple and elegant room. A desk with a banker's lamp sat under the window, and a low bureau with an attached round mirror was near the door. The empty wardrobe indicated Ann's new roommate must not have arrived yet.

She was alone. After the rush of the last few hours, the solitude felt good. Her suitcase and purse rested on the top of the bureau where the bellhop had left it. There was also a copy of the Post Intelligencer, the newspaper she'd seen in the cab earlier. Would she have enough time to get some lunch before her meeting with Dean Prouty? Ann glanced at her watch. Thirty minutes. The apple and cheese her father had given her before she left Wenatchee on the train that morning would have to do.

Ann brought her lunch and the newspaper over to the desk and sat down to read.

"'Working Wife' Loses U.W. Faculty Berth." The headline caught her eye. It went on to say that a semi-secret "Anti-Nepotism" resolution had been put in place at the University of Washington to address the financial woes of the Great Depression. The university administration said that "those married women who were on the payroll whose

158

husbands were able to support them should be dismissed from their positions." At the request of Governor Martin, a list had been compiled of "married women and relatives" and "married couples" at the university.

Eager to keep the new policy as quiet as possible, University President Sieg had only informed the department chairmen. A favorite tenured professor from the art department, Lea Puymbroeck Miller, had been away on sabbatical for the past fifteen months, studying abroad. During that time, she'd married zoology professor Robert Miller. She'd been unaware of the resolution and was promptly fired upon her return. It caused an uproar among the staff and students who loved her.

A chill ran through Ann's body as she took a bite of her apple and continued to read about the ridiculous and unfair resolution. She wanted a career and a family someday. Hopefully, the situation at the university was an isolated case. Why couldn't a woman have both? Aunt Rose was unmarried and, therefore, safe, but how would she react to the news?

For now, Ann had to get to a meeting with Dean Prouty. She was excited to learn which classes she would take that fall and get settled into college life. She tried to put the disturbing article out of her mind as she looked in the mirror and carefully applied her favorite red lipstick.

She wore a brown silk dress with white bands on the cuffs and collar. Her slim figure was enhanced by the feminine style of the dress—a nipped waistline and tea-length skirt. Two-tone, high-heeled Mary Jane's completed the ensemble. Her dark wavy, shoulder-length hair was pulled up with a tortoiseshell comb on one side, and the only jewelry she wore was a gold Cartier wristwatch that had belonged to her mother. She'd traveled in the same outfit, but there was no time to change. Hopefully, it would do.

Later that afternoon, Ann walked into the lobby of Hotel Sorrento and sighed with pleasure. This stunning place would be home for an entire year!

The meeting had gone well, and Ann was smiling. Classes would start in two days. Some of the other women were arriving now too. Maybe her roommate was here. What would she be like? Would they become friends? The concierge stepped out from his podium to hand her a piece of paper with a phone message from Aunt Rose. She was back in Seattle and wanted to meet Ann in the Fireside Room of the hotel at seven that evening.

After a much-needed time of rest in her room, a change to evening clothes, and some time spent exploring and marveling at her new surroundings, it was time for Ann to meet her aunt downstairs.

"Hello, darling. I have someone I want you to meet!" Aunt Rose waved to Ann as soon as she stepped into the Fireside Room. A tall, handsome man stood beside her. Ann approached the couple and leaned toward her aunt to kiss her cheek. Rose beamed as she turned and placed her hand through the crook in the man's arm.

What was that sparkling diamond doing on her aunt's left finger?

Find it on Amazon or read it Free on Kindle Unlimited

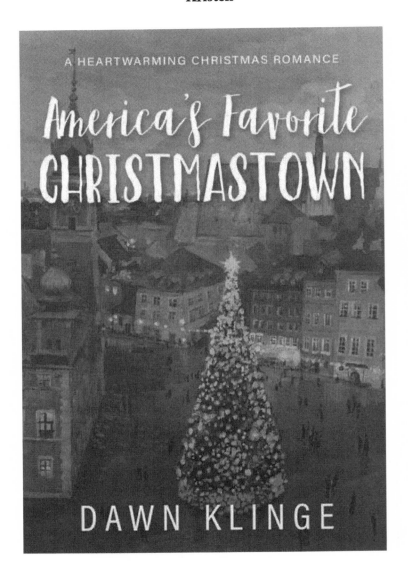

Will going home help Alexis re-discover the true spirit of Christmas?

If you enjoyed this book, please consider leaving a quick review and telling your friends. This helps more than you know and is so very appreciated!

Let's keep in touch!

You can sign up for my free newsletter at

www.dawnklinge.com

You can also find me on Instagram @dawnklinge

Thank you for reading and for spending your valuable time reading this story. You make the hard work of writing a book worthwhile, and it is an honor to get to share my words with you.

With love,

Dawn

Made in the USA
Columbia, SC
15 August 2024

40494655R00102